The Elves of Vulgaard:
Dragon Games

R. A. Douthitt

ISBN-13: 9798739985552

The Dragon Games is a work of fiction. References to real people, events, establishments, organizations, or locales are intended only to provide a sense of authenticity and are used fictitiously. All other characters, incidents, and dialogue are drawn from the author's imagination. The perspective, opinions, and worldview represented by this book are those of the author and are not intended to be a reflection or endorsement of any publisher's views.

Printed in the U.S.A.

Other books by R. A. Douthitt:

The Dragon Forest
The Dragon Forest II: Son of the Oath
The Dragon Forest III: The King of Illiath
The Elves of Vulgaard Book One: The White Wolf
The Children Under the Ice
The Children in the Garden
The Children of Manor House
The Cafeteria Club

DEDICATION

To my son, Nathaniel Scott Douthitt
"Nate"
My favorite dragon rider.

PROLOGUE

In the days of the Darkness that had enveloped the land of Vulgaard from beyond the Cardion Valley of Illiath, right to the entrance of The Dragon Forest, the people did their best to live, hope, and dream.

Though many wondered, no one dared to ask about the cause of the Darkness that hardened the land, making the harvest nearly impossible.

Deep inside their hearts and minds, they knew.

Long before the Gaarden family claimed a plot of ground in the green hills of Glouslow, a man rose to power by bestowing gifts upon the rulers of kingdoms. This man, Lord Bedlam, graced with mysterious powers that even most wizards did not comprehend, was able to fool these rulers into trusting him. He beguiled them with his words and treasures, gaining more power and wickedness with each year.

And the Darkness spread.

But one king, Alexander of Illiath, withstood Lord Bedlam's requests and tricks, standing firm in protecting the one thing the narcissistic Lord wanted more than anything in the land.

The Dragon of the Forest.

All the rulers from Vulgaard to Illiath, and the lands stretching to the eastern shore, knew that the scales of the elusive Dragon of the Forest were more powerful than any weapon forged by man, dwarf, or elf. Any army that marched with weapons made from the scales would be invincible.

When asked to invade the forest, slay the Dragon, and obtain the scales for himself, King Alexander declined and defended the Dragon Forest from Lord Bedlam's puppet rulers.

Lord Bedlam's plans to destroy the Dragon of the Forest continued, and his dark spell on the land covered the regions like a dark blanket, smothering all life, intermittently.

The evil Lord wanted the people to suffer so they would finally cry out to him for relief. But the people held fast. They made a way to live through the Darkness, astounding the evil Lord, whose heart grew in wickedness right along with the spell he had cast.

When the only son of King Alexander was abducted and brought to a mountain prison run by one of Lord Bedlam's stooges, Valbrand, those who had longed for a chance to defeat the evil Lord saw a sign. Like a ray of hope cutting through the Darkness, a plan was set in motion.

A possibility arose, but one obstacle stood in the way.

Without the trust and help of the dragons, there could be no victory. But man had long ago destroyed that trust by harming the dragons, enslaving them, and using the kind, intelligent creatures as mere beasts of burden.

Only one people understood the dragons and respected them for what they were. The Elves of Vulgaard worked with the dragons of all the regions and spoke their language. A mutual affection had developed and prospered.

It would take the courage and ingenuity of the elves to include the dragons and accomplish the plan of destroying Lord Bedlam, ending his spell over the land.

And it would begin with Kieron Gaarden, an elf from Glouslow.

CHAPTER 1

It didn't appear right away to Kieron that his dragon, Vâken, was signaling to turn, but once the massive oak tree came into his view, Kieron pulled up on the reins in time to avoid collision.

But the hearty laughter of his brother, Théan, could not be avoided. The eldest of the Gaardœn siblings, Théan never missed a chance to annoy his younger brother.

"Impressive!" Théan shouted as he and his dragon raced past. And for a moment, Kieron felt proud that perhaps his skills had impressed his older brother. But the smirk on Théan's face revealed the sarcasm.

All Kieron could do was pat his dragon on the neck and thank him for preventing another humiliating story from being told around the dinner table back home.

"Extra treats for you, boy," he said.

Vâken landed gracefully and champed on the bit in his mouth. Kieron leapt off and removed the bridle and saddle from his dragon. "There you go, boy. Freedom at last, huh? Excellent practice today. I think we're almost ready."

Vâken's light green scales sparkled in the sunlight as he shook the sweat from his body. A smaller Draco, Vâken stood only slightly taller than his master, but his wide wingspread and long neck helped him glide through the air. Kieron liked that Vâken had smaller spikes along his back that reached to his tail.

"Yes," Kieron said as he stroked the smoother scales on his dragon's snout. "We're almost ready."

"Ha!" Théan laughed. "Hardly. In fact, you've so much more to learn about dragon riding."

Kieron frowned as he watched his brother land nearby, surrounded by admiring fans. The elation on their faces made Kieron grimace with scorn.

"One day," he whispered to Vâken, "That'll be us. We'll be winners of the Dragon Games and have all the adoring fans."

Vâken shook its head and began munching on the moist green grass beneath his claws.

"You must be thirsty. Come on. Let's get you to the cave where you can eat, drink, and rest. You deserve it."

"Well done, Kieron!" Kealy shouted as she approached. A few years older and wise beyond her years in dragon riding skills, she remained Kieron's best friend and confidant. "You both looked amazing out there."

"Still struggling with navigating those trees, though." Kieron shrugged.

"You'll improve with more practice. Trust me." Kealy pulled up her tunic to reveal a large bruise on her ribcage. "I know what I'm speaking of. If you don't have a few bruises, then that means you aren't practicing hard enough!"

Kieron winced. "Looks painful."

"Dragon riding *is* painful. Anything worthwhile is painful. That's what makes you stronger. You'll find out soon enough, my friend." She patted his back. "Let's get something to eat."

Together, the friends led their dragons to the cave that was used as a stable for the dragons. Kealy, tall and thin with long white hair parted on the side, was pretty for being so tough and rugged. She had become like an older sister to Kieron ever since Aislinn died.

Aislinn.

She was everything Kieron wished he could be. Brave, strong, and an excellent dragon rider. She was well on her way to winning the Dragon Games and a place on the queen's Dragon Riders. She and her dragon, Gwyn, were the best. Even Théan couldn't catch her, and he knew it. Kieron's older sister had also been his instructor. Accurate in archery, Aislinn came close to winning the archery portion of the Dragon Games. But close isn't good enough. She had trained continuously in the woods near their home, but still took the time to help Kieron train.

"Open your chest wide," she had advised him during an archery lesson. "Pull the arrow back and hold your breath." Kieron could still sense her presence, standing behind him as his instructor and protector.

"Aislinn"

But Aislinn was gone. Forever.

Kealy came alongside him and encouraged him to enter the tournament. She and Aislinn were inseparable and when Aislinn died, Kieron understood why Kealy took him under her wing as a little brother. It was as if she wanted to do it for Aislinn, in her memory.

Kealy's beast, Söen, a mid-sized Wyvern, squawked and chirped as she made her way to the waiting stall, careful not to drag its impressive wings on the ground. Walking required some clever maneuvering for Wyverns, due to their having only two large legs. This made them resemble birds of prey more than the reptiles that scurried along the desert landscape outside the forests of Vulgaard.

"Söen sounds more like a bird than a ferocious beast." Kieron laughed.

"She may sound like a bird with her little squawks and chirps, but just know that she is a fearsome dragon in the air, able to swoop and strike even the most elusive enemy." Kealy shook a finger at Kieron. "I know of what I speak."

Söen stood proud, with her small head held high. The cool breeze from the mountains brushed her face and she sniffed the air. Tiny wisps of smoke rose from her nostrils. The sunlight danced on her dark scales and leathery wings. Her long thin tail swished along the ground.

"I know, I know. I have seen you both in the air. You will win the tournament again this year. I can feel it." Kieron watched as Söen made her way past him. "You both have worked hard all summer." Kieron raised the wooden beam used for a doorway to Vâken's stall and let him in. "Now, with the event just weeks away, I am even more convinced of your victory."

"And I of yours, Kieron. I know you are teased about your youth and size, both you and Vâken. But I have seen much improvement in your skills and techniques. I really have." She hand-fed her dragon some fish taken from a nearby barrel.

"Now that's a bit of humor much needed on such a hot and trying day as today," Théan chortled.

"Shut up, Théan." Kealy frowned. "You've had your victory and adulation today. Aren't you satisfied enough for the day? Can't you let us alone in peace?"

"Just ignore him. I always do." Kieron fed his dragon from the barrel of fish, too.

"What a pathetic sight you both are. Trust me, dear Kealy. Kieron is too young and too small to participate in this tournament, let alone win any prizes. And his dragon? Don't get me started on it."

Kieron's eyes became mere slits and his jaw clenched so tightly, one could hear the sound of his teeth grinding together. "Now look here. I don't mind you belittling me. But you leave my dragon alone!"

Seeing her friend seething in anger, Kealy stepped between the brothers. "Let's go inside and have some grub, shall we? The heat has affected more than our practice. It seems our tempers are flaring as well. Come!" She ushered them to their respected corners of the cave. "You eat in peace over there, Théan, and we'll enjoy our lunch over here." Kealy waved her hand.

But Théan snorted. "No, thanks. I'm taking my leave and heading to the lake for a swim."

Kieron and his dragon watched Théan fly away on his dragon into the bright orange sky, a sky still untouched by the Darkness that hovered over the nearby regions. Vulgaard suffered only minor effects of the spell cast by Lord Bedlam. The ground hardened, frustrating the farmers like Kieron's father.

"Well eat up, and then we'll head out to my home for dessert. How does that sound?" Kealy grinned.

Kieron smiled at the thought. Kealy's home was bright and cheerful, thanks to her kind parents. "Sounds like a plan."

He continued to feed his dragon. After they finished lunch, they left the cave and headed down the path toward Kealy's home.

A quaint little cottage with a thatched roof, the home was one of Vulgaard's oldest. Passed down through her family's lineage, Kealy knew it would one day be hers.

"Hello! Welcome." Her mother stood in the doorway, waving her guests into the abode. A pudgy woman with messy hair, Kealy's mother had a contagious smile even though she had such a large family to look after. "Lunch is already served. Better hurry before the others gobble it all up."

Kieron raced past her, knowing what it meant to not eat due to many greedy siblings ravaging the food before him. He gladly grabbed a plate of meats and fruit before snatching few biscuits.

"I know practicing for the tournament causes a hearty appetite. Don't worry. There's plenty for all," Kealy's mother said.

"Thanks, Ma." Kealy pecked her mother's cheek as she passed by.

"You'd better pay attention to how to serve twenty guests, Kealy. Once you marry and bear children, this will be your task soon." Her mother wiped her hands on a cloth.

Kealy rolled her eyes and sat down next to Kieron. "Whatever you say, Ma."

Kieron knew home and hearth was not in Kealy's future. All she ever spoke of was riding with the Queen's elite group, The Dragon Riders. The way she'd described it to him made him want to set aside life as a farmer and try out himself. But he knew his chances were slim. He'd have to win in the Dragon Games and gain the attention of the Prince of Vulgaard if he was to try out. Not Kealy. She was good. Good enough to win a place in the elite group. Being a farmer's wife and mother to many children just wasn't in her future.

"Kieron!"

"What?" A few crumbs flew from Kieron's mouth.

"You just ate lunch in the cave. Now you're eating again?"

"He's a growing boy," Kealy's mom said. "Let him be."

Kieron grinned.

"Well, hurry up. We've a lot of work to do, and you need to practice a few moves," Kealy ordered.

"Ha ha," Kieron mocked.

After lunch, Kieron mounted Vâken, heeled the dragon's ribs, and together they dove off the cliff. As the force of the wind pushed him backwards, Kieron relented to the force, spread his arms wide, and grinned. Pulling up on the reins just in time, Kieron tugged and Vâken swooped up, skimming the river water with its feet.

"Yes!" Kieron shouted. He heeled Vâken's side again and the dragon shot straight up like he was going after prey. Kieron gripped Vâken's saddle with his thighs, tugged on the reins, and motioned for the dragon to twirl in mid-air. When it reached its zenith, the dragon hovered in the air for a second or two, allowing Kieron a glimpse of Vulgaard from the air. The river sliced through the valley and tiny villages peppered the countryside. He even saw some smoke rising from chimneys in the distance. And way off in the distance, emerging from the mountainside, stood the Palace of Vulgaard in all its splendor. It sparkled like a jewel. Kieron smiled at the sight and then he and Vâken did a free fall. Kieron's insides floated within him, giving him a tingling feeling inside. He laughed as they fell from the sky like a shooting star. He leaned back and closed his eyes, relishing in the feeling of flying.

A jerking motion stirred him out of his trance and he opened his eyes to find his dragon racing toward a tree growing out of the mountainside. It was soon caught up in branches of the tree on the side of a cliff.

"No!" Kieron shouted. He used his arms to move branches away from his face. Vâken roared from frustration. He pulled and tugged on his wings and clawed at the branches with his front and back legs. Kieron did his best to calm Vâken while he broke branches, trying to free them both.

"*Hang in there!*" Deep inside his head, he heard his sister, Aislinn's, voice. Instantly, he was reminded of that awful day the previous summer…

"*Very funny!*" *he shouted to Aislinn when he and his then dragon, Pegasus, were trapped in a cliffside tree.* "*No more jokes. Just help me. I don't think this tree will hold us much longer, and its wings are stuck.*"

Kieron remembered watching his sister dismount her own dragon, Gwyn, and climb onto the tree.

"*What are you doing?*" *he had shouted at her.*

"*I'm getting you out of yet another bind. That's what big sisters do,*" *she said as she reached for a branch. Once she had found her footing, she climbed further onto the tree.* "*Let me break a few of these branches and let your dragon loose.*"

A loud crack was heard.

Kieron shivered as he remembered that day.

"*The tree can't hold all of us!*" *Kieron had shouted at her.* "*Get out of there, Aislinn!*"

But she ignored him and continued twisting and pulling branches away from Kieron and Pegasus. "*Almost there. Just a little bit more, and you're free!*"

"*Aislinn!*" *he had cried to her. But she ignored him.*

Snap!

Vâken's roar woke Kieron from the painful memory. His eyes grew large and he pulled out his knife to cut away at the branches that trapped him and his dragon, but Vâken spewed fire and freed them. The two shot out of the tree and flew away toward home.

Once on the ground, Kieron leapt off Vâken and collapsed to his knees, clutching his chest, desperately trying to breathe.

"What's the matter? What happened?" Kealy asked as she hopped off her dragon and rushed over to Kieron's side. "All I saw was Vâken trapped in the tree, some fire, and then you two diving toward the earth." She cupped her friend's face in her hands.

But it was all Kieron could do to not hyperventilate. He closed his eyes and took slow, deep breaths. "I could see…I could see Aislinn, and she was—"

"Shhh, it's okay. Say no more." Kealy hugged him. "When I saw you both trapped in that tree, I had a feeling you were thinking about it."

Kieron wiped his eyes and quickly stood. "I heard her voice."

"It's okay."

"I'm alright," he whispered. "Come on. Let's go back out there for another try."

"You sure?" Kealy watched him approach his dragon.

"Yeah." Kieron took the reins into his hands and hopped onto Vâken's saddle. "Everything's fine."

"You're late. Where have you been?" Kieron's father shouted from behind the fence that surrounded the pig sty.

"Sorry, Father." Kieron led Vâken by the reins into the stalls, carved out of a cave.

"You've chores to do before supper," his father barked. "Did you hear me?"

"Yes sir." As Kieron closed the gate behind Vâken, he sighed. Deep down inside, he dreaded coming home after practice. Without Aislinn, it was just a house on the farm. He tossed some hay into the stall and watched as his dragon, his friend, chomped.

"Want some fish, boy?"

But Vâken shook his head, circled around a couple of times, then plopped down onto the hay with a loud harrumph.

"I can take a hint." Kieron smiled and entered the stall. He gently removed the bridle off the dragon's snout, patted it on the head, then left Vâken to nap.

Inside the house, the kitchen was cool and dim, not bright and warm like at Kealy's house. Kieron's home smelled of cooked fish and bread.

"Hello, Kieron," his mother said without looking at him. "Here's some supper for you." She placed a bowl of fish soup onto the table and set a basket full of bread next to it. "Do you want some milk to drink?"

But before he could answer, the front door flew open.

"He'll eat after his chores." His father picked up the bowl and placed it onto the stove top.

Kieron stood with his back toward his father. His hands formed into fists.

"Now get to work." His father brushed by him and removed the bottle of milk from the counter. He gulped it down. Kieron watched with a clenched jaw. Shouting at his father wouldn't help, and he knew it. But he also knew what the matter was. Before Aislinn's accident, he and his father fished in the pond every afternoon. There was laughter and games inside that house. Fun games, played by the fire after dinner, that made them laugh until their bellies ached. Games that he usually won. Now, he and his father hardly spoke, and Kieron knew why. His eyes welled with hot tears. He wanted to shout it, but he knew he couldn't. *You blame me for her death, I know it.*

"What's the matter with you?" his father said. He squinted his eyes. "Well?"

Kieron wanted to say it. The words burned in his mind. But he knew he couldn't do it. "Nothing." He blinked back the tears. "Nothing is wrong."

"Well then. Go do your chores, starting with that dragon stall. It reeks."

His father slammed down the bottle and raced past Kieron without looking at him.

His mother approached with her arms out, but Kieron stepped away from her embrace. "He hates me."

12

"No, he doesn't. Don't say such things."

"It's true. He hates me."

She reached up to touch his cheek, but he turned away from her.

"And I know why."

Aislinn.

Kieron ran outside and headed to the cave where Vâken napped.

For it had been Aislinn who taught Kieron how to saddle a dragon, bridle it, and handle it with care.

She had also showed him how to speak to dragons, using dragonspeak that all elves knew but many had forgotten.

"Speak to them in their language, and you'll gain their trust," Aislinn would tell him.

But Kieron was timid to try it. He didn't want Théan to tease him about his dragonspeak. With Aislinn's encouragement, he finally tried it and gained the trust of Pegasus and now Vâken. Aislinn was his older sister, but also his best friend.

When she died, all life went out of their home like a candle blown out by the wind. All that remained were the fond memories, rising up into oblivion like the wisps of smoke from the extinguished candle.

"Come on, boy," he ordered.

Vâken hopped up with wide eyes.

"Let's go for another ride."

Escape was all that Kieron had anymore. His home, darkened by the overwhelming cover of loss like a thick wool blanket, no longer felt safe.

Being in the sky on the back of a dragon was the only safe place.

In the air, Kieron motioned for Vâken to dive into the White Forest. As they did, the cool moist air brushed his face, calming his spirit. He closed his eyes and inhaled the fresh scent of pines. Out there, nothing could bother him. The forest was his true home. Flying through the sky was the best way to get his father out of his mind. This was his favorite place in the whole world with his most faithful friend in the whole world. Ever since Théan had taken Pegasus for himself, Vâken was all that Kieron had. Aislinn had picked him out from a bundle of newly hatched dragons, but Théan had said it was too small and scrawny to be any good to anyone.

Kieron knew better.

Vâken pulled up, stirring Kieron. He tugged on the reins and landed the dragon next to the pond.

"Hey!" He heard a shout coming from behind. He turned to see his friends coming toward him.

"What are you doing here?" Kealy asked. She tilted her head. "Escaping chores again?"

Kieron ignored her and led Vâken to the water for a drink.

"Did you get in trouble again?"

Theyer, Kealy's younger brother, crossed his arms. "I bet you're in big trouble. You know, your brother was just here."

Kieron jerked his head around. "He was?"

"Yep. We saw him grab a sack full of fish he'd caught. He flew on his dragon's back toward your farm. I bet your father is ordering him to come find you right now." Theyer laughed. "Now you'll really be in trouble."

"Shut up, Theyer." Kealy shoved her brother aside. "Go on home, you little pest."

"I don't care if Théan comes to get me. We'll just fly away." Kieron picked up a stick and drew in the mud. *I'll fly away and never come back to that awful place.*

"What are you doing out here, anyway? The sun's going down soon. You need to get home, finish your chores, and eat supper. You don't want to give your father any more reasons not to let you enter the tournament." Kealy stood watching Kieron draw a dragon in the mud with a stick.

"I know, I know." He exhaled a few bangs out of his eyes.

"Did you tell them about what happened today?" she asked.

"I never tell them anything anymore. Every time I bring up training or dragon riding, Father changes the subject back to farming. He thinks I'm going to be a farmer, and Théan is the one who will be in the Queen's Dragon Riders." Kieron pouted. "Just because Father was one of the Queen's soldiers once doesn't mean he knows everything. They might pick me."

"Of course." Kealy bit into an apple.

"They might want a smaller rider."

"Sure." Kealy winked at him.

Kieron pictured the impressive team of riders, led by the Queen's brother, Prince Thætil, flying high above them. The rows of Elfin warriors, dressed in their white leather armor and silver shields was quite a vision. "I saw them once, the Dragon Riders." He looked up at Kealy and smiled.

She smiled back. "I know."

"It was here in the White Forest. They were returning home from battle and—"

A dragon roar from deep within the trees interrupted Kieron. He dropped the stick in his hand and stood. Kealy turned toward the sound.

"Did you hear that?"

They stood completely still, holding their breath.

Another roar sounded.

"What was that?" Kealy asked.

"Kealy"

"It was a dragon," Theyer replied with eyes wide with fear.

"That didn't sound like any dragon from around here," Kealy said. Her eyes filled with fear, too.

"Much bigger than the dragons from here." Kieron began to walk toward the sound, but Kealy grabbed his forearm.

"Where are you going?"

"To find out what's going on," he answered and pulled away from her. "Come on."

"Oh no you're not."

"Come on, chicken." Kieron chuckled.

Kieron felt that only Kealy understood how important it was for him to leave home and do something on his own. He was not a farmer and she knew it, too.

"Maybe we should head home and tell the grown-ups about it, you know?" Theyer rocked back and forth. "I don't think we should investigate."

"Stay here, then." Kieron continued on.

"Kieron." Kealy watched him then glanced over at her brother, who continued to rock back and forth, wringing his hands. "I can't go with you and leave my brother behind. There's only a few more minutes of sunlight left."

"Go back, then." Kieron motioned for Vâken to follow him. The loyal beast obeyed.

Once inside the trees, Kieron tip-toed toward the noise. The shouts of men and the crack of a whip were heard, echoing within the trees. The hairs on his arms stood. "Something's wrong," he whispered to Vâken. The dragon gurgled.

"Shh," Kealy ordered. Kieron turned to see his friend and her little brother following after him. "They'll hear us."

They stooped down behind some large rocks and spied what was happening in the clearing.

Several men had surrounded a rather large Draco tied with ropes. One man whipped the dragon as another approached with a bridle.

"It'll burn him alive," Kieron whispered.

But the man who held the whip pointed to the side. Kieron raised his head to see a baby dragon being held down by another man, with its snout wrapped with ropes as it struggled to breathe. The leader of the men pointed to the baby dragon while sneering at the large Draco, obviously its mother. Her dark gray scales and yellow eyes gave her an ominous appearance that matched her wrath. A guttural growl came from her throat as she glared at the men threatening her baby.

"She had better not spew fire or they'll kill her baby," Kealy whispered.

"Barbaric." Kieron narrowed his eyes. "We have to do something. And we have to do it now. We have to do something to stop them." Kieron removed a knife he had attached to his belt.

"You're joking, right?" Theyer asked.

"I think he might be serious," Kealy replied.

"I am serious. You can help me or stay here, but I'm doing something about this."

They sat helpless as they watched their friend crawl away from the rock.

"Get moving!" the leader shouted to the other men pulling the Draco toward them. "We're late. Valbrand expects these dragons at the prison by morning. Move!"

Kieron turned to Kealy. "They're taking them to the prison?" he whispered. He swallowed the anger rising in his throat. "Whatever for?"

Kealy shrugged. "Get back here." She waved at him. "Before you get caught."

"Captured!"

CHAPTER 2

K ieron edged toward the scene, crawling on his belly like a snake. The dead leaves crunched, making a noise loud enough to make the dragon's ears twitch, so he stopped.

"It's going to burn you!" one man shouted to his leader, still threatening the dragon's baby.

"No it won't. It's very smart, this one. She knows we'll kill her baby if she puts up a fight." He narrowed his eyes and stared into the dragon's dark yellow eyes, wide with fear.

"Let's go, then," the man said. The mother dragon watched as he motioned for the others to lift the baby and place it into the wagon.

With more whip cracks, the men directed the dragon to begin following them along the path leading out of the forest. Kieron watched and felt the earth shake with each step of the massive beast.

"Now what are we going to do?" Theyer asked as soon as he slid next to Kieron.

"Not sure." Kieron counted the men walking behind the dragon. Three men, each armed with wips and small swords. Two horses pulled the wagon carrying the baby dragon, tied with ropes.

"Hey? What are we going to do?" Kealy asked. She crouched next to her brother and Kieron.

"Let's follow them." Kieron stood up and made his way up to the ridge that overlooked the path the men walked along.

"No, Kieron. It's going to be completely dark soon. There's no full moon tonight. We need to get home, now," Kealy argued. But she followed after him with Theyer close behind her. "Kieron!"

"Shh!" He lifted his finger to his lips and then nodded toward the path. "They'll hear us."

Kealy rubbed her forehead. "Kieron, stop. This is crazy. We

cannot follow these men. We don't even know where they are headed." She took hold of her brother's arm. "Go to Kieron's home and tell Théan what's happening.

"But…" Theyer winced.

"Go, now!" Kealy nudged her brother and watched him crawl away, climb back up the hill, and disappear.

Kieron crouched down and moved along the ridgeway, never taking his eyes off the men. "I know where."

Kealy came alongside him. "What?"

"I said I know where they are taking this dragon." He placed his knife back into the sheath attached to his belt.

"How could you possibly know?" Kealy placed her hands on her hips. "You're just a farmer elf."

"I overheard my brother telling my father about the prison inside the Ranvieg mountains. These men here are the Riders of Rünbrior. Look."

He pointed the emblem on the banner held by one of the Riders.

"That's the prison banner. I know it is." Kieron squinted his eyes.

"How do you know?"

"There's a rumor that the prison has an arena inside, where the dragons fight." He pointed to the dragon being led out of the forest. "I'm going to follow them and free those dragons."

"An arena?" Kealy whispered.

Vâken snarled, and silver smoke snaked from his nostrils.

"You ready, boy?" he asked.

"You can't possibly do this." Kealy grabbed his forearm. "If they are truly Riders of Rünbrior, they will kill you if they catch you."

Kieron stared into her eyes.

"And if you don't care about that, then consider that they'll kill your family, too." The corners of her mouth turned down.

He pictured the men riding to his home. But then the dragon roared, shaking him out of the thought. "I can and I will. You head home if you like, but I can't. I have to do something to free those dragons. Otherwise they'll be forced to fight in the arena and possibly die." Kieron took off down the ridge. He motioned for Vâken to fly off, knowing he'd meet his dragon on the ground.

"Wait! Kieron, don't do this. It's insane," Kealy cried after him.

21

∽

At the bottom of the ridge, Kieron saw that the men had turned west, heading out of the White Forest and into the sunset. The wagon the horses pulled cast a long shadow.

Vâken landed with a grunt.

"Shh, boy," Kieron said as he approached the dragon. He stroked its neck.

A few stones rolled down the ridge and Kieron glanced up to see Kealy sliding down the edge of the ridge.

"I see you decided to come along." He smirked. "I thought you'd join Theyer and run home for momma."

"I sent Theyer back to get your brother."

"You didn't really, did you?"

"I did."

Kieron shot her a harsh look.

"You don't know what you're getting into."

"Come on, then." Kieron motioned for her to follow.

"I won't go any further unless you have some sort of a plan."

"A plan?" He tilted his head.

"Yes! What's the plan? I'm not just going to follow you to that prison."

Kieron scratched his head. "Well, I was going to sneak up to the wagon and cut the ropes with my knife. Once the baby is free, then that momma dragon will burn them all to ashes."

Kealy's eyebrows rose.

"Well?" he asked.

"Sounds like a plan. What do you need me to do?" Kealy asked.

"Cause a distraction. When I get close to that wagon, you ride Vâken above them and then swoop close. Not too close, because they may have crossbows." Kieron began his trek toward the wagon.

"Okay." Kealy turned to Vâken. "Are you alright with this?"

The dragon snarled again.

"Alright then." Kealy rolled her eyes. "This should be interesting."

Kieron snuck up behind the wagon, doing his best to stay out of sight of the men walking on each side of the wagon. They had covered the wagon with a canvas tarp, but he could hear the baby dragon's muffled cries coming from underneath.

"Shut that thing up!" shouted their leader. Kieron leapt behind a tree as one man hopped onto the wagon and kicked the baby dragon, under canvas tarp.

"Keep quiet in there," he said.

Kieron scowled. Once the man jumped off the wagon, he continued following behind it.

The mother dragon lumbered along with her head hung low. Kieron's heart ached at the sight.

The cry of Vâken above made the men glance upward. That was Kieron's signal to jump onto the wagon. As the men pointed their arrows and crossbows at Vâken hovering above, Kieron leapt onto the wagon, quickly cut the ropes, and shoved the baby off the back of the wagon. It rolled a few times and stood, blinking its green eyes at Kieron before it cried out for its mother. She jerked her head around to where her baby's cries came from. Kieron rushed behind a tree and watched the scene, hoping she didn't see him.

Some of the men shot their arrows at Vâken. Carrying Kealy made Vâken's movements awkward, but he dodged the arrows successfully.

The mother dragon heard her baby cry again. She searched the area and when she saw the baby dragon standing alone in the woods, she stretched out her wings, tearing apart the net they had thrown across her back. She inhaled and spewed her fire over the men, engulfing them in flames.

She whipped her head and tail around, hitting the wagon, sending it flying into the trees, where it splintered into pieces. Kieron dove out of the way just in time to miss the splinters of wood flying through the trees like shrapnel.

"Whoa," he murmured at the sight of the powerful dragon's wrath.

The horses scrambled to their feet and galloped away to safety, reins and harnesses flopping behind them.

Kieron rolled out of the forest and leapt to his feet. His eyes met with the mother dragon's glowing yellow eyes. Her sides went in and out with each breath, while wisps of smoke rose from her nostrils. Her snout curled into a fierce snarl that caused Kieron's knees to shake. He lifted his hands in surrender, hoping she would show mercy since he had just rescued her baby. It scrambled over to its mother's snout, crying out to her. She nuzzled her baby and stared deep into Kieron's soul.

They stood silent for a moment, Kieron frozen with fright.

"Ish leon di mythriel don il ilion," he whispered to the dragon and her baby. "Uth vas al uthrien."

Kealy landed Vâken nearby, being as quiet as she could so as not to startle the beast.

The mother dragon tilted her head and sniffed Kieron's quivering body. "Uth vas al uthrien," he repeated to her, trying his best to remain perfectly still as not to upset her.

After a few moments, he nodded at the dragon and she lowered her head. Kieron hoped the movement meant she would spare his life. He took a few steps back. "Ey ithriel."

"What's this?" Kealy whispered as she watched her friend speak to the dragon in a language it understood.

The three of them watched the beast take her baby in her jaws, flap her wings, and fly off into the lingering slivers of sunlight.

∽

Kieron fell backwards and exhaled, not realizing he had been holding his breath the entire time. He clutched his tight chest.

"Kieron!" Kealy ran over to him. "Are you alright? You weren't hurt, were you?" She touched his arms and legs to check for broken bones.

Kieron stared straight ahead with his mouth open.

"Hey, are you okay? Come now, we must get you home." Kealy grabbed his arm and helped him stand. She brushed the dirt off his trousers. "You're a mess."

But when she tried to lead him to Vâken, Kieron resisted.

"What? What is it? Are you hurt?" she asked.

He shook his head.

"Then what is it? Let's head home."

"No," Kieron said.

"What do you mean, no?"

"I'm not heading home just yet." He made his way over to Vâken and took the reins into his hands.

"Kieron! What do you mean?" Kealy ran to him. "Where are you going? And when did you learn to speak to dragons?"

He shook his head. "I…I don't know. Aislinn taught me. I simply spoke to her like I do to Vâken, and the dragon understood."

"I don't understand." Kealy frowned.

He studied his worried friend's face. "I spoke in dragonspeak. Didn't you understand what I had told her?"

Kealy grabbed his arm. "No. I didn't. What you had spoken to that dragon was unlike anything I have heard."

Kieron thought about it. "All I know is that Aislinn taught me to speak to dragons. She said all elves can speak to them if we try."

"Kieron, where are you going? You did what you said you were going to do. It's time to go home."

"Not until I find out what they do with dragons inside that

25

prison."

All Kealy could do was watch him fly off into the star-filled violet sky.

She ran back to her dragon, Söen. "Let's follow him."

In the air over Vulgaard, Kieron gently kicked Vâken's ribs to make him go faster. He flapped his wings even harder, sending them higher into the air until they soared close to the mountainside.

"There!" Kieron shouted as he pointed to a cave in the side of the mountain. Below, he could see the tiny glow of the torches of men on their way out of the prison entrance. He sensed they were probably heading out to search for the missing men and their prize dragons. He circled above them for a moment and then set his sights on the prison entrance. A wide entrance guarded by many men, he knew it would be too dangerous to head inside through that entrance. "Come on." He tugged on the reins to turn Vâken to the left. "Let's head to that small cave."

"Hey!" Kealy shouted, teeth chattering in the cold night air.

"I thought you were heading home?" Kieron asked.

"I thought about it, but…" she replied. "I can't let you go in there and get killed. Someone's got to save you from yourself."

Kieron rolled his eyes. "Come on, then. Let's head to the caves."

The two of them flew close to the mountainside, inspecting the many caves, hoping one led into the prison.

A stream of fire startled them. "Whoa!" Kieron shouted and pulled Vâken back, away from the deadly stream of yellow fire.

When the fire stopped flowing, they blinked their eyes to see where it had come from. Before them stood the mother dragon at a cave entrance. Behind her, on the ledge, stood her baby dragon.

Kieron held up his hands and Kealy directed her dragon to hover behind Vâken.

But the mother dragon didn't seem angry. She jerked her head toward the cave entrance.

"Do you think she wants us to land, too?" Kieron asked Kealy.

"I don't know. Maybe it's a trap?" she replied, keeping her eyes on the mammoth dragon.

"Let's see what happens." Kieron motioned for Vâken to land.

Kealy followed, and the pair landed directly in front of the massive beast. She glared down at them and lowered her head. She sniffed Vâken's snout first and then Kealy's dragon, Söen.

Their heads tilted back and forth and they grunted in their own language.

"Looks like they understand each other," Kealy whispered and slid out of the saddle. Kieron did the same and inched his way into the cave.

"I think we're safe here," he said as he inspected the dark cave. "Let's go inside."

But the large dragon roared and stopped them in their tracks. Kealy and Kieron fell to their knees in fear.

"We're dead," Kealy cried. "She's going to burn us alive."

"Shh," Kieron ordered. "Not another word."

The beast turned her massive body. Her tail swished right by the youths. Before they knew it, they were face to face with the dragon's snout. Kieron could smell the sulfur coming from her nostrils.

"What do we do now?" Kealy whispered.

"Bow," he said. "Ithrien il ish an anil…"

Kealy obeyed. Kieron hoped their submission would make the dragon spare their lives.

Instead of burning them, the dragon nudged Kieron, sending him backwards. He looked up at her. She nudged him again, this time causing him to fall onto Kealy.

"Hey," Kealy said.

The dragon glanced over to another cave entrance and then she returned her fierce gaze to the youths before her.

Kieron looked behind her at the other cave entrance. "Oh!" he said. "I understand!"

"Understand what?" Kealy asked.

"Come on!" He stood up and headed toward the mountainside. "This way."

"What?" Kealy hesitated. "Are you crazy? You don't actually expect us to scale that rock wall over to that other cave, do you?" She glanced down. "It's probably a thousand feet down!"

The dragon snarled at Kealy. Thin lines of silky smoke rose from her nostrils.

"Kieron"

"Ahem." Kealy smiled warmly at the dragon. "If that's what we're supposed to do, then that's what we'll do. It's probably better to fall off this cliff than to be burned alive."

Kieron easily scaled the rocky mountainside. "Just follow me. Put your feet where I place mine, and same with my hands."

"Why are we going to that other cave? I'm sure this cave leads to the prison." Kealy did her best to grip the ice cold rocks with her hands. Snow covered the ledges, making them slippery.

"I think that cave is hers. It probably has her nest inside and that's why she doesn't want us to go inside," Kieron said.

"But we won't bother her eggs," Kealy said.

"She doesn't know that. Besides, after what she's been through, I don't think she's in a trusting mood."

"I suppose you're right," Kealy said. She glanced down at the icy rocks below.

"Don't look down!" Kieron had reached the cave entrance and held out his hand. "Take my hand and I'll pull you over."

Once they were safely inside the cave, they waved to the mother dragon, who gladly hosted, Vâken and Söen inside her cave.

"They'll be safe and warm in there while we head inside," Kieron said. "Come on!" He motioned for his friend to follow him inside the cave, but stopped.

Kealy stood with her arms crossed and mouth tightly closed.

"What is it now?" Kieron asked.

Kealy's eyes narrowed. "I'm not going anywhere until you tell me your plan."

"My plan?" he cocked his head. He hadn't really thought up a plan yet.

"Yes, your plan. I'm not budging until you explain it." She tapped her foot. "When I woke up this morning, I had no idea I'd be in a cave on the Ranvieg Mountains considering a rescue attempt of dragons inside a prison. So, if you want my help, I'd like to see some sort of a plan."

"Well..."

"You've got one, don't you?" Kealy leaned toward him. "What's going on inside that head of yours? What's gotten into you?"

"I have a plan, it's just that..." he lied. "Why I just need a stick, and I'll draw it in this dirt here."

Kealy reached into her trouser pocket and pulled out a pouch. She pried it open and removed some matches and twine. She found a rather large branch and broke it in two. Next, she wrapped the twine around it and lit it on fire to make a torch.

"Fire light!" Kieron said. "Great idea. Here." He yanked off a sleeve of his shirt and wrapped it around the branch.

"Let's see it then." Kealy waited.

Kieron took the stick and drew his plan. "We'll go through these tunnels until we reach the prison cell blocks. I've heard there are separate cells for the dragons. Once we find one, we'll break in and rescue the dragons. One by one, we'll go into each cell and—"

"Be burned alive!" Kealy shouted. "You're crazy. I'm going home."

"What? No, you don't understand. I heard some say the prison guards remove the glands within the dragon's throats so they can't spew fire." Kieron lowered his head. "My brother told me."

Kealy covered her mouth. "They do? How are the dragons supposed to protect themselves?"

"They can't. All they can do is claw at one another and bite each other in the arena." Kieron shook his head. "You see? This is why we have to save them from the grotesque battles."

Kealy thought about it. "I don't know, Kieron."

"What's the problem?" He placed his hands on his hips.

"Once we free a dragon, then the guards will be after us. If that dragon can't spew fire, then we'll have no protection from their swords and arrows as we flee."

"No, we're fast. We know these tunnels. We'll slip back into these tunnels with no problem. Once we lead them to that mother dragon, she'll burn them alive. Trust me."

"I don't know these tunnels." Kealy glanced around. "I know *you* don't know these tunnels. Only your brother seems to know, and he's not here. Besides, I don't believe your brother. He tells some rather tall tales. I seriously doubt he was ever inside this prison."

"Trust me. Together, we'll sneak into a cell, talk to the dragons, and tell them what we're doing there. I just know they'll follow us out of this hell hole to freedom," Kieron explained. "They'll lead us out."

"Talk to them?" Kealy asked.

Kieron waved his hands. "You've got to trust me. Dragons understand us more than we understand them. You should try to talk to Söen."

Kealy shook her head. "I told you before, I never tried."

"Trust me, all elves can talk to dragons. We'll try it and see what happens. Let's go."

"You don't know it these dragons will trust you." Kealy grumbled. "You'll probably say something that angers the dragons and we'll be killed." She kicked a small stone. "It's insane!"

"We've got to try."

Kealy exhaled. "I supposed you're right. What chance do those poor dragons have?"

"Exactly!" Kieron patted her on her shoulder. "I have a knife. Do you have yours?"

She shook her head. "No, I left it at home."

"Okay, well, stick close to me, and I'll protect us." Kieron removed his knife from his belt. "Ready?"

Kealy pursed her lips and exhaled, again. "I have a feeling I am really going to regret this."

∞

The two youths made their way deeper into the cave, using the torch to light their way. As they stepped over the dried bones of various animals, it dawned on Kieron that dragons had been there before them. Hungry dragons.

"Creepy," Kealy said as she passed a few skeletons.

"Look at that." Kieron pointed toward the ground.

Kealy lifted the torch to have a better look at what he pointed at. There, lying on the damp ground, were three skeletons of dead men.

"Uh oh." Kieron gulped. "Their leg bones are missing."

"Maneaters," Kealy replied in a quivering voice.

"Just keep going…"

Soon they could hear the clanging sound of metal and the rattling of chains.

"Hurry up!" They heard a guard shout.

Kieron motioned for Kealy to douse the torch. She dropped it onto the muddy ground and stomped on it. Then, the two of them belly crawled to where the tunnel ended.

"Oh wonderful." Kealy groaned.

"What is it?"

"My new tunic is covered with mud."

Kieron rolled his eyes.

The cave opened out to where dozens of boys, chained together, marched in line. The heat from fires hit Kieron's face like a slap. He ducked back down.

"What's happening?" Kealy asked.

Kieron motioned for her to see for herself. Kealy craned her neck and peered out. The heat made her squint her eyes and quickly lower her head down.

"Where are they taking them? They look so young, not men like I thought they would be," she said.

"I don't know, and I don't care about that. All I care about is finding the cells that hold the dragons." He scooted away into the darkness.

"What are you morons doing?" a voice came from the cave.

Kieron turned in time to see Théan and Geraint, his friend, kneeling just outside the tunnel.

Kieron covered his eyes, "Oh no."

"Quiet," Kealy whispered. "The guards will hear you."

Théan pointed at Kieron and waved him over. "Get over here."

Kieron shook his head.

"Now." Théan narrowed his eyes. "Or else." He ran his finger over his throat slowly.

Kieron shook his head.

"Just go grab him so we can get out of here," Geraint said.

"Shh!" Kealy ordered. "Look, just leave him alone."

"Our father sent me here to get him and bring him home. That's what I'm going to do." Théan began crawling over to Kieron.

"No, I'm not leaving here without the dragons." Kieron turned and headed along the ledge, doing his best not to be seen by the guards and prisoners below.

His boots scattered a few pebbles, sending them bouncing off the wall of the cave. His eyes widened with fear.

One of the boys marching below glanced up. His eyes widened too, once he spotted Kieron. He opened his mouth to speak, but stopped, as though he realized what was happening.

Kieron lifted a finger to his lips and the boy prisoner nodded.

But Théan and Geraint scooted toward Kieron with scowls on their faces.

Kieron leapt onto another ledge, knowing his brother's larger body wouldn't be able to make it onto the narrow ledge. He leaned against the wall, stuck out his tongue at Théan.

"He has no idea what he's doing," Kieron heard Théan say right before he slipped and fell to the ground.

Théan and Kealy lurched forward to try and catch him, but it was no use. Kieron landed hard with a thud, scattering the marching boys.

"Guard!" one boy shouted and pointed at Kieron. Another boy raised his shackled hands and covered the boy's mouth.

The other boys stopped marching to see what had happened. Their mouths dropped open when they saw Kieron, struggling to stand.

"What are you doing here?" one boy said. He stood in front of Kieron and motioned him to move out of the light.

"I'm came here to rescue the dragons enslaved inside this prison." Kieron rubbed his ankle.

"Are you crazy?"

"Yes, he is," Kealy said, climbing down the wall. She landed near Kieron and helped him to stand.

"Who are you boys? Where are they taking you?" Kieron whispered.

"We were captured and brought here to train for the arena." One boy nodded toward the others, who were gathered around, staring at Kieron.

"What's your name?" Kieron asked.

"Eagan of Durishire," he replied. "We were participating in the Dragon Games and lost. But before we could return home, the Riders captured us and our dragons, forcing us to work inside this prison and train to fight in the arena."

"That's terrible,'" Kealy said.

"What's going on back there!" shouted a guard.

Kealy and Kieron scurried away, hiding behind a large barrel.

"Get moving! All of you." The guard raised his whip, threatening to beat the boys if they did not march forward.

Kieron and Kealy watched as the line of chained boys, made their way through the tunnel toward yet more rooms carved out of the mountain and lit with torches. The line of boys seemed never-ending.

"This is madness." Kealy stood with her hands in fists. "We need to do something. They're abducting boys to be slaves. I thought this was a prison?"

Kieron tried to stand, but his ankle ached.

"Are you alright?" Kealy helped him.

"Yes." Kieron stood, watching the line of prisoners disappear into the tunnels. "Let's get moving." "But what are we going to do?" Kealy pointed to his ankle. "You're hurt, and Théan is on his way down to get you. He's determined to take you back home."

Kieron shook his head. "He'll have to catch me first. Come on!"

CHAPTER 3

Kieron used his hands to guide him along the rock wall through the blackness. Too proud to admit even to himself that he had no idea where he was going, he hoped the tunnel lead to somewhere. The sore ankle screamed with pain, but Kieron did his best to ignore it.

"Up ahead." He motioned to Kealy. "I hear something."

"Sounds like metal clashing." She followed closely behind him, wincing and plugging her nose. "And it definitely reeks of dragon dung."

They paused when they heard a loud roar and swords clashing echoed through the caves.

"Training must be up ahead. Let's go see," Kieron said.

"You're joking, right?" Kealy's mouth dropped open.. "We've no weapons and you want us to stroll right in there where men are fighting each other with swords?"

Kieron sighed. Something inside him told him there was a better way. "No. You're right. It's too dangerous. Let's keep going to another part of the training area."

Another dragon roar shook the walls.

"I say we go this way. The dragons are below, and that's where we can free them." Kieron made his way toward the sounds.

Kealy swallowed hard. "You want us to go *toward* the sound of a ferocious dragon?"

"Yes." Kieron belly crawled toward the fire glow, listening for the sound of guards. "I understood what the dragon said."

Kealy cocked her head. "What did it say?"

"Stay back," he replied. "Or else."

"Do you suppose it's talking to us?"

"Or it was talking to whomever is standing before it with a sword," Kieron explained.

When he reached the tunnel's end, his mouth dropped open. Directly below him were three young dragons, chained to the cave wall. They tugged at the chains attached to their back legs, bloodied from pulling and tugging. The dragons, lithe Wyverns with long necks and tattered wings, hung their heads down. Kieron noticed their sides were so thin, the deep indents of their ribs could be seen. A few scales were scattered on the ground. He'd learned in school that sick and weak dragons can lose their scales.

Kieron's heart sank within him at the sight of such young dragons so defeated and starved. "Look at them."

Kealy approached, frowning at the sight. "What horror."

Hoping their fire glands had been removed already, Kieron scaled down the rock wall, making sure to remain in the darkness and out of the torch fire's glow. When he landed on the ground, he scanned the area for any sign of the guards, only then motioning to Kealy. "It's safe."

"Maybe the dragon was warning us to stay away?" Kealy slid down the wall, careful not to startle the weary dragons. A wooden stool sat in one corner along with a pipe, but no swords were in sight.

Kieron removed his knife and crept toward the dragon cages. "I don't know. But I've got to do something." The sound of the dragons groaning made his stomach turn. He spotted the blood on their legs where the metal cuff gripped them too tightly.

Metal chains, Kieron thought. He glanced at his useless knife.

"That knife won't do you any good in here, boy." A gruff voice came from behind him, making Kieron jump and the dragons growl.

He gripped his chest and fell backwards onto Kealy.

The man came out of the darkness and leaned over them.

"Who are you?" The man squinted. "What are you doing in here?"

Kieron and Kealy backed away.

The man jabbed his finger at them. "I asked you a question."

"I'm Kieron…and this is Kealy…"

"You're elves and definitely not prisoners," the man said. He inspected the pointed ears, white hair, suede trousers, and tunic Kieron wore. "Fine stitching on that garment. Sewn by your mother, eh?" The man chuckled.

Kieron looked left and right for a sign of escape, but he knew the only way out would be to climb back up the rock wall to the tunnel.

"Don't think about it," the man said. "The guards will be here soon."

"Please, mister. Don't let them catch us here," Kealy pleaded. "We only came here to free the dragons. Please."

Kieron approached him with hands out. "They need to be freed."

The man laughed. "Don't you worry yourself, boy." He reached out his hand once again. "The name's Dangler."

The man had a scruffy beard the color of fall leaves sprinkled with some gray and twinkling eyes that seemed to be like pale blue ice. Dangler wasn't much taller than Kieron. He suspected the man was part dwarf.

"Hello. I'm Kieron Gaardoen." He moved his bangs away from his eyes. "Yes, I am an elf from Glouslow, just outside the White Forest."

"I know where that is." Dangler scowled. He picked up his stool and plopped it down in front of the dragon cage. From inside his pocket, he removed a carrot and fed it to the beast. It hobbled over to the carrot, dragging its hurt leg behind it. "That's a beautiful land with tall trees and grasses."

"It used to be." Kieron glanced down at this feet.

"What do you mean?"

"Ever since the Darkness, not much grows. It's very hard for our people to farm," Kealy explained. "But we were able to plant a crop this year. It will be time for harvest soon…if the Darkness doesn't spread."

Dangler leaned back. "Some of the best fishing is out there in Glouslow."

"That's true." Kieron pictured the pond near his home. "My father and I would…" His voice trailed off.

"Would what?"

With a sigh, Kieron thought about fishing with his father and riding dragons with Aislinn. "I mean, my sister and I would train for the Dragon Games near that pond. The trees thin in that part of the forest, so we can practice the obstacle course portion of the tournament."

"You there!" came a shout from behind them. A guard appeared in the entry way. "Get those dragons ready for battle or put them down."

"Aye," Dangler replied without turning around.

"And get these prisoners to their cells!" The guard sneered at Kieron and Kealy.

"They're helping me with the dragons."

The guard spit onto the ground, spun around, and left just as quickly as he appeared.

Kealy gripped Kieron's arm.

"Don't worry," Dangler said. "I can have helpers."

Kealy exhaled.

"So you long to participate in the games, eh?" Dangler studied the two elves before him.

Kieron nodded and thrust out his chest. "All elfin boys do."

"And girls. Well, we used to want to participate." Kealy crossed her arms.

"But not anymore?" Dangler ate a carrot.

"No, not after we found out what happens after the games," Kealy shouted.

Dangler listened.

"Those prisoners out there told us they were abducted after the games. Is this true?" Kealy approached him.

Dangler nodded. "Aye. It is."

Kieron pointed toward the dragons. "And they capture dragons against their will! How can you be a part of this?"

Dangler hesitated. "So you're the great dragon hero, are ya?"

Kieron raised his chin. "Yes."

"You really think you can free all the dragons within these walls?" Dangler made his way over to where Kieron stood. "You're a bit young, aren't ya?" He looked him up and down.

"No, I am not. I am exactly twelve and I made it this far, didn't I?" Kieron straightened up to appear taller.

"Hmm..." Dangler studied him.

Kieron turned toward him. "I may be young and small, but I can still do something to help those dragons."

"A dragon rider, are you?"

"Yes! And we're both good. Very good." Kealy placed her hand on Kieron's shoulder.

"I see."

"Being small is to my advantage." Kieron pointed his finger at Dangler "You see, my smallness makes it easy for me to navigate through those low lying branches. I get in real close to the dragon and we fly as one."

Dangler grinned. "Seems you've got it all figured out."

"I do."

"What do you know of the Darkness?" Dangler's eyes narrowed to mere slivers.

Kieron thought about it and a chill rushed over his body. "I know it's been around since before I was born."

"Yes. A long while before you were born, and it'll take something much larger than you and I to rid Vulgaard and Thèadril of the Dark spell that has the land held hostage." Dangler shook his head.

"I don't know anything about that. All I know is we're here to free these dragons. Now, let them go!" Kealy insisted.

"It'll take something much larger than us and you…exactly what did you mean by that?" Kieron stepped close to Dangler. "Who are you, anyway?"

A grin slowly crept across his face. "I'm the dragon master here inside this prison. And you two probably have the best timing of anyone in all the land."

Kealy and Kieron looked at each other.

"What do you mean?" Kealy asked.

Dangler tossed more carrots into the cages and the dragons munched on them. "You know of the kingdom of Illiath?"

"King Alexander's kingdom? Yes, of course." Kealy tilted her head. "Why?"

Dangler made his way away from the cave opening and waved his guests over. Kieron began following after him, but Kealy stopped him.

"Be cautious. We don't know this man. This could be a trap." Kealy glanced around the room. "We don't have much time to waste here before Théan finds us," she whispered.

"I want to hear what he has to say." Kieron whispered back.

The two youths stood followed the dragon master in the dark corner.

"I've been hoping and wishing for a sign. I do believe you two are the sign I was hoping for. A prisoner, Ethan of Riverdale has been fighting in the Great Arena with a former Royal Knight. Together, they have been victorious, gaining the trust of the wardes," Dangler explained. .

"And?" Kealy leaned in close.

"This boy, Ethan…he is too good a fighter to be just a boy from a small town. I suspect he might be Prince Peter of Illiath." Dangler wrung his hands as though nervous.

"What?" Kealy leaned back. "That's ridiculous."

"I have my suspicions." He asked them to lean in close. "I heard that the prince was abducted by the Riders of Rünbrior and was brought here."

"How can that be? King Alexander would have rescued him by now," Kieron said.

"All I know is that this Ethan fights in the arena with a former knight of King Alexander and they are winning. Ethan is the best dragon fighter I have ever seen within these walls." Dangler looked left and right.

"The prince?" Kealy crossed her arms.. "Of Illiath? In here? Fighting dragons?"

"Shhh…" Sweat appeared on Dangler's forehead. "It is a secret."

"Why hasn't every ruler in the land descended upon this mountain prison and rescued him?" she asked.

"The Darkness." Dangler hobbled down the darkened hallway.

Kealy shook her head and took Kieron's arm. "Let's get out of here now. This man is crazy. We're wasting time. I'm sure the guards are on their way."

"What caused the Darkness anyway?" Kieron shouted after him. "My father would never tell me when I asked him."

Dangler disappeared into a room for a few seconds.

"Now's our chance. Let's go." Kealy started to walk away.

Dangler reappeared, carrying a large object covered with a tarp. "That's because the Darkness is alive. It knows. There are spies everywhere. When you see a crow fly overhead, you can bet it's Lord Bedlam's minions, spying on you. Your father's wise not to speak of it."

"Dangler, Dragon Master"

"Lord Bedlam?" Kealy glanced all around the room, rubbing her arms. "I feel a chill."

"There are no crows in here. Tell, us. What happened?" Kieron studied the object in Dangler's hands.

Dangler blew his bangs out of his eyes. "Long story, boy. You ever hear of the Battle for Illiath?"

Kieron nodded his head.

"Well, that was all a ruse." Dangler glanced left and right. "Lord Caragon was just a puppet, used to distract King Alexander and the other rulers. The real evil remains."

"Yes…" Kieron thought back to the time of the war.. "I suspected as much. I remember overhearing my father and brother discussing it one night when they thought I was asleep."

"And the warden of this prison is just another one of Bedlam's puppets. They're everywhere. He puts them in power and pads their pockets with coin to make them do whatever he asks of them. That's what keeps the Darkness over the lands. Nothing will grow like it did before until it's finally gone for good."

"Why does Lord Bedlam have so much power and influence?"

Dangler chortled. "Because foolish men gave it to him. Years ago, he wasn't the strong leader that he is today. He bewitched men and women–and elves–into giving him power and influence. He has a way with—"

"Words?"

Dangler shook his head. "No…with dragons."

Kieron's eyes grew large.

"He speaks their language and knows what they're thinking." Dangler used his finger to tap his temple. "It's as if he's one of them."

"He speaks dragonspeak? I can speak dragonspeak." Kieron narrowed his eyes. "Is Lord Bedlam an elf?"

"No one knows what he is." Dangler raised an eyebrow. "Except the queen's wizard. He knows."

"I was told only elves can speak the language of the dragons." Kieron raised his chin, proudly.

"So you understand them, eh?" Dangler fiddled with his beard.

"He's very good with dragons." Kealy nudged Kieron. "Tell him.".

The caged dragons in the other room moaned.

"Those dragons must be freed. They're dying. Kieron can help them. How can you just sit here and allow them to die like this?" Kealy asked.

"Listen here, I've been training dragons and fighters for the arena since long before you were born. Since before your fathers were born. Unfortunately, as long as there are dragons, there'll be dragon games in this arena."

Kieron sighed. "Please, mister. You've got to help me free them."

Dangler studied Kieron and Kealy. "Trust me, I will. There is a way." With that, he removed the tarp to reveal a magnificent sight. In his hands was a sparkling dragon's scale, large enough to shield a grown man's body from neck to knee.

Kealy and Kieron stumbled backwards, with mouths open.

"What is that?" Kieron leaned in toward the scale.

"This…is all that matters." Dangler's eyes sparkled like the scale in his hands. "It is the scale from the Great Dragon."

"Of the forest?" Kealy asked with wide eyes. She covered her mouth.

The caged dragons growled and flapped their wings.

"How…when…*where* did you get that?" Kieron raised his hand to touch it, but Dangler quickly smacked his hand away.

"It is time. If you can speak to the dragons like you say you can and if this Ethan of Riverdale is indeed the prince, we just might be able to put an end to this wicked place once and for all." He covered the scale with the tarp again. . "If you will help me."

"You, too?" Kealy narrowed her eyes. "You mean, *you're* also a prisoner here?"

Dangler glanced away and returned the scale to the room.

Kieron followed and inspected the room in which they stood. There were dull swords stacked against the wall, a few shields were scattered nearby, along with a few helmets. Water dripped down the stone walls and the bones of small animals littered the cages where more weary dragons stood.

"So, you've been forced to train the fighters and dragons?" Kieron said.

"Aye." Dangler moved toward Kieron.

"How sad." Kealy frowned.

"But for the first time in many moons, I have hope. Together, with you and the Prince of Illiath, we will be successful." Dangler clapped his hands together.

"I don't know…" Kealy hesitated. "It sounds dangerous, and I'm responsible for him. His older brother is on his way to find him, and if I don't bring him home…If I don't get home soon, I'll been in so much trouble." She wrung her hands together, glancing at the tunnel they came from.

Dangler rolled his eyes. "My dear," he began. "I don't think you understand what we are dealing with here." He gestured toward the entrance. "The only way any of us is getting out of this wretched place is to escape. That's it."

"My brother knows how to break in and break out. He's done it before." Kieron grinned.

"Your brother was allowed to leave; that's the only explanation. Trust me. There are spies throughout the land. Valbrand and his Riders know what all of you mountain folk are up to. In fact, I suspect they know he is on his way to rescue you. So, you'd better decide what you're going to do right away."

Kieron looked at Kealy. "You mean, my brother is a spy?"

"No." Kieron shook his head. "That can't be true."

Dangler stacked the helmets and swords against the wall.

Kealy stroked Kieron's arm. "It's alright."

But Kieron had a far off look in his eyes. "I don't believe it."

"It makes sense. It would explain why he entered the prison and then was allowed to leave it." Kealy forced a weak smile. "You know? And it would explain why he's always so angry all the time."

But Kieron shook his head. "I refuse to believe it."

Dangler spun around. "I know it's hard to believe, but you have to trust me."

Kieron leered at the broken man before him. "You don't know my brother!"

"Shhh!" Kealy tried to cover his mouth. "There are guards out there."

"Look, there is no way the Riders of Rünbrior would have let your brother leave this prison unless they wanted to use him to gather information about the townsfolk." Dangler found a small wooden stool and sat on it.. "It's how they work."

Kieron thought about it. "I want to…I mean, I want to trust you." He glanced over at the dragons in the cage. A bit of life and light had come to their eyes. He approached them. "I must remain inside here to help these dragons escape." He reached out to them. "An anil uthra," he whispered to them. Their tales swished back and forth in the dirt. "I will help you." He turned to Kealy and took her arm. "But you should leave when Théan comes for us."

She yanked her arm away. "And leave you here with this old man, these dragons, and the guards? Are you mad?"

Dangler raised an eyebrow.

"I'm in this to the end. We will simply tell Théan to return home and inform our families that we are now part of the plan to free all inside this dungeon." She furrowed her brow as if she didn't believe her own words.

"Kealy…" Kieron shook his head. "You are right. Your parents are probably very angry. You need to go home and now!" He gently shoved her toward the tunnel.

"But I can help you train!" She pushed back. "You know I am better than you are in flight."

"Hey!" Kieron placed his hands on his hips.

"Listen, you two, we need to get a move on with this plan. First thing you'll need to do is get Valbrand's attention."

"Valbrand?" Kieron asked.

"The warden." Dangler shuffled toward the wall and searched for helmets that would fit his two visitors.

"The warden?" Kealy's eyes grew large.

"Yes. He is the one who decides who fights and who…remains chained to work the mines." Dangler turned a sword over in his hand, weighing it.

"How do we do that? How do we gain his attention?" Kieron asked.

"How?" Dangler winked and tossed a helmet to Kieron. "By winning in the arena."

Kieron held the metal helmet in his hands.

"Here." Dangler tossed a helmet to Kealy. "Try this on."

"Winning…you mean fighting other prisoners?" Kealy gulped. "To the death?"

Dangler rolled his eyes. "No. Flying dragons."

Kieron smiled.

"Well, Kieron can do it. And with my help, he will win." Kealy nodded.

"But how will winning lead to our escaping with the dragons?"

Kieron cautiously approached the dragons in the cages, making eye contact with them.

Dangler watched as Kieron, with his trembling hand outreached, gently stroked one of beast's snout. It closed its eyes as though enjoying a soft, caring touch for a change. Kieron looked into the sad eyes of the beasts, longing for the touch of someone who cared.

"These beasts trust you." Dangler uncovered a wooden barrel, reached in, and removed a fish. He tossed it to the dragon. "We will need their trust if we are to ask them to help us escape."

"When I think of how these intelligent and gentle creatures were captured and beaten into submission just to fight in the arena, it sickens me." Kieron turned to Dangler.

"I know," he replied. "If you can she can win in the smaller arena, Valbrand will order that you fly dragons in the Great Arena so he can win gold coin from your victories. You will have the chance to use your dragonspeak to alert more dragons…the *big* dragons. We will need them to fight off the guards."

"Won't that be…dangerous?" Kealy chewed on her upper lip. "Maybe I should go back home."

"Dragon flying is all about skill. What you'll need is speed and accuracy to win. You both tell me you are good. Well? Are you?" Dangler smirked.

"Yes," Kealy replied.

"Well, then. Be victorious, earn the trust of the dragons, speak their language, and when Ethan of Riverdale reveals that he is Prince Peter, we will make our escape."

Kealy paced back and forth. "If he is the prince."

Kieron turned towrd her.

"What if he isn't?" Kealy asked Dangler.

"Yes, what if he is just Ethan?" Kieron stood next to his friend.

"He is the prince. I am willing to bet everything on it." Dangler shook his finger at them.

"Even our lives?" Kealy shook her head.

"Look, I gave that boy my book, The Dragon Chronicles, because I sense something in him. He is the one."

Kieron and Kealy looked at one another.

"The Dragon Chronicles?" Kealy asked.

"I have been working with dragons for many years. I have chronicled all that I know about them into one book. I trust Ethan so much, that I gave him the book so he can learn about them. He is special."

Kealy took Kieron's arm. "Then let him risk his life. We're leaving." She began to drag Kieron away from the dragon cage.

"No, wait..." He resisted her. "I can't leave."

"He wants us to take too many risks, Kieron." Kealy grabbed his forearm again.

But Kieron freed himself and returned to the cage. He patted the dragon's head. "I care about the dragons,," he said to them. "Il ierie elsin longin. Il ierie."

The dragon perked up and its tail swished left and right.

Dangler, watching the scene from the corner of the room, grinned.

Kealy smiled at Kieron. "I know you do, but..."

"Ish elion, theiyn anal nyrthra, ish ilnion," Kieron said.

"These dragons understand you" Dangler said.

"All dragons understand the elves," Kieron corrected him. He stroked the dragon's snout. "Everything will be alright." The dragon closed its eyes and leaned into the soft stroke on its scaly skin.

"But not all elves can speak dragonspeak," Kealy explained.

"They could if they tried." Kieron said to Kealy without turning away from the dragon.. "It requires a soul for dragons."

"How do you know all this?" Dangler asked.

"By talking to dragons. They'll teach you everything you need to know." Kieron motioned to the caged beasts.

"Come on, then," Dangler said. He made his way over to the cage, removed his set of keys, and unlocked the large padlock on the door.

Kieron stood off. "What? Are you making us part of the plan?"

"Aye," Dangler said. He approached the wounded dragon and unlocked its hind leg from the metal cuff. "But it means you both will have to stay here inside these walls for a bit longer."

"How much longer?" Kealy rubbed her arms, nervously.

"You'll train in the smaller arena, participate in a tournament, win, and I promise you, Valbrand will command that you be brought to him." Dangler held onto the collar around the wounded dragon.

"But..." Kealy's eyes met Kierons. "What if this Ethan isn't the prince?"

Dangler shot her a stern look. "He is."

"How do you know?" Kieron asked.

"Why would a royal knight purposefully be caught and brought inside here to fight alongside Ethan?" Dangler carefully walked the dragon out of the cage. "I tell you, it's him."

Kealy shook her head. "Kieron…"

"We have to help these poor creatures." He helped the dragon walk.

"The risk, it's too high!" Kealy rubbed her forehead as if it ached. "I followed you in here, but now you are asking too much of me."

"We can do it, Kealy," Kieron said. "I promise you, I will do it. I will win and earn the chance to speak with the larger dragons. I'll gain their trust. I'll tell them of the plan to escape. You'll see. They want to leave this horrid place and return home."

Kealy stared into the weary eyes of the dragon, being led out of the cage. She watched as Kieron fed it more fish.

"Oh all right." She agreed and made her way over to the dragon. As she carefully lifted her hand to touch it, the beast jerked its head away. "It's okay, boy," she said. "I'm here to help you. We both are.

CHAPTER 4

The idea of training several dragons for the games had never occurred to Kieron in all his life. All he'd ever worried about was making sure Vâken understood the maneuvers required of the tournament. But after working with Dangler's dragons for two days, Kieron knew he'd have to train them on more than just maneuvers. They would need to know strategies, how to anticipate the competition moves, and all the many ways to score the most points.

Dives, recovery, swooping, and all the other moves would have to be accomplished if they were to win the attention of the warden. But ultimately, Kieron knew he would have to earn their trust if he and the others were to escape.

No pressure. He scratched his head. *I just need to escape from here to save all the dragons from being killed inside this prison. And if I fail, my family will suffer from the Darkness, coming war, and the evil Lord Bedlam.* His head throbbed *No pressure at all.*

After a couple of times in the arena training with the dragons, Kieron and Kealy felt it was time to show Valbrand their skills. But Dangler had insisted they needed a few more prisoners to assist them.

Dangler had arranged for boys to join in the training. "The guards were reluctant at first," he had told Kieron. "But I told them Valbrand had ordered it."

"And they believed you?"

"Of course." Dangler had grinned. But Kieron and Kealy remained a bit skeptical about the plan.

"This way." Kealy led the other prisoners and Kieron down the darkened corridor. Stalagmites spiked from above them, water dripped down the cave walls, and the musty smell grew thicker. "Dangler trains in the smaller arena."

Kieron's back ached from sleeping on the ground, and his stomach growled from hunger. He and Kealy had slept in a small room near the dragon cages inside Dangler's cave. They survived eating his rabbit stew, hard biscuits, and drinking his bitter grape juice. It was no banquet feast. Dangler's cooking made Kieron appreciate his own mother's dull cooking all the more. He thought about home, his siblings, the farm, and even his father as he made his way through the dank tunnels. But the training in the small arena had been a glimmer of hope. Dangler's dragons were smart and eager to learn. It was as if they understood this was their chance to escape.

Approaching guards alarmed the boys and they froze in place. Kealy held out her arms to steady them. With Kieron in the back of the group assuring them, they remained still

"Move!" shouted the guard from behind.. Kealy motioned for the boys to continue down the corridor.

"This way, boys." Kealy directed them.

"Move it, you scum!" the guard shouted as the group began to edge forward, causing some of the smaller boys to cower. "Valbrand might let you train in here, but if it were up to me, I'd have you all mining in the caves, turning big rocks into stones night and day!"

The boy prisoners cringed.

"It's alright," Kieron whispered to the shaking prisoners. He helped a couple of them make their way down the hall. The shackles around their ankles made it difficult to walk.

Once they made it into the arena, Kealy led the chain of prisoners over to the dragon stalls. "This is where you will care for and watch the dragons as we fight in the games. Kieron and I will signal you when we need a replacement dragon to ride. Understand?"

But the boys froze, with eyes wide open, in the presence of the beasts.

"Don't worry. They won't hurt you." Kealy offered a smile.

But the boys stood far off just in case.

Kieron made his way over to the dragons, reached up, and stroked their necks. Once the prisoners saw that the dragons were, in fact, tame, they made their way over to them..

"I haven't named them yet," Kieron said. "I need to see them fly first. But they won't harm you if you are kind to them. Understand?" It had been days since Kieron had left Vâken in the cave with Söen, Kealy's dragon. He hoped Vâken was alright, but he couldn't dwell on it. He had a job to do and he needed to be successful so he could rescue all the dragons. Deep inside, he knew he'd see his little dragon again.

One boy reached up to touch a dragon, waiting in the stall. It snarled a bit, but didn't move away. Once the boy's hand touched the slick gray scales, he smiled and the dragon remained cautiously still. With spikes down its back, the dragon looked fierce.

"See?" Kieron said. "They won't harm you until you harm them."

"I see." The boy's smile lit up the room.

"What is your name?" Kealy asked as she led the others to the dragons in their stalls.

"I am Yon." He bowed his head. "Of Rivertown."

"Well, Yon. You are about to learn how to ride dragons." Kealy nodded to him.

"Now what, dragon boy?" a boy named Thyler said to Kieron Some of the other boys laughed.

Kieron raised an eyebrow. "Excuse me?"

"You heard me." He spat on the ground. "Working with dragons is easy. What makes you the expert?"

Kieron knew boys like Thyler back home. They were arrogant and cocky because they thought they knew it all. "I am a dragon rider. But you will clean their stalls."

Thyler chortled and crossed his arms across his chest. "I don't think so. What makes you think you are the only one who can work with dragons?"

Kieron stepped aside. "Be my guest."

The boys turned their heads and waited for Thyler to do something.

He adjusted his belt, snorted, and walked toward the dragons in their stalls. Some were gray, others dark gray, and one had greenish scales. Once Kieron stood before them, he raised his arms and yelled like a madman, scaring them out of the stalls and onto the arena floor. Dirt and pebbles flew into the air from the flapping of wings and stomping of feet.

The boys coughed and gasped from all the dust in the air.

"See?" Thyler said. "It's easy. These dragons fear me and will do whatever I ask."

"You didn't ask them to do anything. All you did was frighten them." Kieron shook his head. "Go ahead. Try asking them to return to their stalls."

Some of the boys snickered. Thyler sneered at Kieron.

"Well?" Kieron cross his arms across his chest. "Go ahead."

Thyler shot him a harsh look and approached the dragons. As soon as he did, they flew off like birds evading a predator. They squawked and flapped their wings.

"Well?" Kieron asked again.

Thyler tried again to round them up. He waved his arms into the air. "Get over there!" he shouted at them. But the frightened dragons roared at him and snarled, revealing their very sharp teeth. Thyler retreated in defeat, hiding behind a boy much smaller than himself.

Kieron made his way over to the brood of dragons, cowering together for protection. He felt sorry that they were so afraid. "Anathra vestuth, ish al ieron." He set out his palm for one dragon to sniff. The other dragons joined in. Some were Wyverns and others were Dracos. One dragon had light green scales like the forest, while another had dark gray scales that matched the rocky mountain terrain. Kieron studied their eyes, necks and bodies. He smiled because these dragons were healthy. "Come with me." He gently waved his arm.

The boys watched as the dragons followed Kieron toward the stalls.

Thyler waved him off. "So, they're following you. So what?"

Kieron snapped his fingers and the dragons stood in a line, in perfect unison. "Elrien, il anu lüth." Kieron bowed and the dragons did, too. Kieron stood with his hands on his hips and grinned at Thyler. "You were saying?"

"What about me?" Another boy stepped up.

"And me?" asked another. "I want to train dragons!"

Kieron laughed. "All of us will soon be flying dragons, battling one another."

"Really?" a smaller boy asked.

"To the death?" Yon asked with a frown.

"No." Kieron motioned toward the guards, taking their positions at the arena entrance and by other tunnels leading into the arena. "In this arena, we will participate in games of skill, such as archery. If we win here, these guards will report to Valbrand and then, maybe we'll fly in the Great Arena."

"The Great Arena?" Yon asked. He shook his head. "I don't want to fly in the Great Arena. Those dragons are much larger than these. We hear their ferocious roars from within the mines."

"Kieron and I will win." Kealy winked. "We just need to train you to ride so you can help us fly the dragons out of here." She, too, motioned toward the guards. "See those guards? You'll need to fool them into thinking we all want to make it to the Great Arena."

Yon nodded. "I see."

"But how?" the smaller boy asked.

"What is your name?"

"Aerin," he said. "Son of Aerderin."

Kieron placed his hand on his shoulder. "Aerin, you are about to see how. Come on. Let's get started. We need to make you all dragon riders if we are to free them."

He led a Wyvern dragon out to the center of the arena and spied a few guards standing by. It used its wings for balance. He then waved over Aerin to bring a saddle with him. Together, they saddled the dragon.

"The strap goes underneath the belly and secures here." Kieron nudged the dragon to raise up, but it refused. "Ish ilerön!" he commanded. The dragon, a Draco, stood on all four limbs, allowing the boy to scurry underneath and secure the strap. "See? This dragon won't hurt you."

Aerin grinned.

Kieron hopped onto the dragon and motioned for Aerin to step aside. "Stand back. Watch and learn."

"Myth rien," he whispered to the beast. "I am telling the dragon that everything is alright. It has nothing to fear."

The boys nodded.

"Can you say it? Myth...reee en."

The boys repeated the saying and all the dragons turned toward them.

"See what I mean?" Kieron motioned toward the waiting dragons.

The boys stood wide-eyed with amazement,

Kieron nudged the dragon's ribs, leaned in close to its neck, and took off. Kealy, on the opposite side of the arena, nudged her dragon and, together, they flew toward Kieron. .

Swooping low to the ground, he grabbed a bit of dirt and tossed it at Kealy's dragon as it approached. To dodge the dirt, the beast flew upward, causing Kealy to pull on its reins.

"So it's going to be like that, huh?" she shouted at Kieron, who winked at her, turned his dragon around, and approached.

The boys alongside the arena clapped and cheered for Kieron.

Kealy removed an arrow from the quill strapped to her back. She removed the bow attached to the saddle and loaded it as her dragon flew.

"Look at that!" Yon shouted. Kealy had impressed the boys with her skill.

Part of the games required shooting an arrow as close to the bullseye of the target as possible while flying the dragon and dodging incoming arrows from the opponent. Kealy's dragon flapped its wings to gain speed, and then it glided smoothly as she took aim.

Kieron and his dragon flew by in time to distract her. But Kealy released the arrow and it hit the target…bullseye!

Her new fans below cheered for her as she landed her dragon.

"Ha!" she said as she dismounted, dusting off her hands.

"A lucky shot!" Kieron hopped off his dragon nearby.

"Wow!" Aerin said as he approached. "I want to learn how to fly like that!"

"And you will. Come, let me show you." Kieron motioned for a boy to bring another dragon out of its stall.

"Impressive," Kieron whispered to his dragon as she panted. "I think I shall call you Fly." He stroked her snout and she closed her eyes and sighed. He admired her amber-colored scales that caught the light. With no spikes down her back, Fly was a smooth ride for Kieron. When she opened her eyes, he noticed they were a pale green. "You're a lovely dragon." But deep inside, he missed his Vâken and hoped his little dragon was safe inside the cave.

Kealy made her way over to him. "Playing dirty, huh?"

Kieron laughed. "Something I learned from my brother."

"Well, it will only get you so far." She narrowed her eyes and nodded toward the arrow protruding from the target. "Skill is what it takes to win."

The boys turned to Kieron and began raising their hands and

hopping up and down, begging to be selected to ride.

"Line up and pay attention," Kieron shouted.

The boys obeyed.

"First things first. These dragons have much in common with you. They were taken from a life and family the loved. Now they are stuck in this prison, trying to stay alive and possibly win their freedom. For the next few minutes, you will show them that you care." Kieron lifted his chin.

Thyler rolled his eyes.

"And if I see any attitude…" Kieron leered at Thyler.

"Why do we need to do any of this?" Thyler whined.

"To show them you care about them." Kieron walked over to him. "These dragons don't trust you, nor do they like you. They told me so."

"Really?"

"Yes. They see men as cruel and barbaric," Kieron said. "Now's your chance to show them that's not true about you. So, you will clean out their stalls—"

"What?" Thyler shouted.

"Without complaining or arguing, or you're out!" Kieron shouted back.

Thyler smirked.

"You'll polish the leather saddles to a shine and feed the dragons their lunch. Now, move it!" He pointed toward the stalls and then made his way over to the dragons. "This will be fun to watch." He winked at Kealy.

Some of the dragons didn't understand, so Kieron told them in their own language.

One by one, the boys moved past the dragons, whispering "Myth rien" to them over and over.

One guard made his way over to them and watched.

Kealy smiled. "Good job," she said to Kieron. Her smile disappeared when she saw the guard standing by. "Get to work!" she shouted at the boys.

The boys obeyed and began to sweep out the dirty hay and replaced it with new hay.

"No need to be so harsh," Kieron said. "They want to do the work."

Kealy nudged Kieron to look over at the guard. He did and then quickly stepped away, motioning for Kealy to follow him.

"Excuse me," the guard said.

Kieron froze.

"You two." The guard walked over to them.

"Yes?" Kealy winced and turned toward him.

"You have a way with the dragons," he said.

"Yes. We have permission to be here, training the boys and—"

"I know." The guard raised his hand. "No need to be afraid. The name's Eckert and I have been observing you. As elves, you can speak to the dragons, yes?"

Kieron nodded.

"I thought so." Eckert turned and nodded toward the other guards who stared blankly at the arena as though bored. "Come with me."

He walked off, but Kieron and Kealy remained with the boys.

Eckert noticed and waved them over to a row of barrels. Kieron shrugged and made his way over to the guard with a cautious Kealy following close behind.

"What is it? Do you want them to clean out these barrels?" Kieron tapped his hand on the lid of one barrel.

"No, listen carefully. You two are working with Dangler. That's good. I have noticed that he also helps a young Ethan of Riverdale to fight in the arena with a traitor knight."

"Yes!" Kieron leaned in. "That is true."

"I know about the plan to help the slaves escape. I overheard Ethan tell Dangler. The plan is a good one but we need the Dragon of the Forest to come help us if we are to make it out of here." Eckert pretended to roll a barrel over to where the dragons were.

Kieron and Kealy did the same.

"The Dragon of the Forest? But I thought it was dead." Kealy helped Kieron move a barrel.

"Get these barrels over there!" Eckert shouted to fool the other guards. "No, Ethan claims that a mysterious White Owl comes to visit him and that is the Dragon of the Forest, guiding him."

Kieron's mouth dropped open.

"So, I firmly believe Ethan of Riverdale is Prince Peter. He was abducted in the desert outside of Illiath. I heard some of the other guards talk about it." Eckert pretended to order the two elves to work.

"Then we have a chance." Kieron turned to Kealy. "If this Ethan is the prince and the Dragon of the Forest is secretly helping him, then we do have a chance to escape."

The corners of Kealy's mouth slowly rose into a smile.

"For now, keep training. Keep working toward the Great Arena and you'll have a chance to work with the large dragons. If we can get them to help, then we all have a chance to destroy this prison once and for all." Eckert shook his finger at them as if scolding them.

"Why are you helping us?" Kealy tilted her head.

Eckert sighed. "I once served as a knight. I have been trapped inside this prison for many years. When I saw there was a chance to destroy it once and for all, I knew I had to be a part of it." He walked away.

"Thank you," Kieron whispered to Eckert as he left.

"Dangler was right. There is a plan in motion. Ethan is the prince." Kealy shook her hands. "Can we stop pretending to move these barrels?"

Kieron took her arm and they returned to monitor the boys' work.

The boys used the oils to polish the saddles and then fed each dragon fish. When it came time to pair up the dragons with the boys, Kieron considered it thoughtfully. A dragon needed to trust its rider. It needed to feel safe if it was to devote itself to its rider completely.

As the boys carefully fed the dragons, Kieron watched the animals to see how they interacted with the boys. A few of them allowed the boys to pet them, while a couple remained timid. Thyler, although he did a good job cleaning out the stall, stood aloof rather than feed any of the beasts. This made Kieron wonder. *Had Thyler been hurt by a dragon at some time? Was he taught that dragons were evil?* It could be that being in prison had hardened his heart. Kieron could definitely understand that. He approached Thyler cautiously.

"Why aren't you interacting with them?" Kieron asked.

Thyler ignored him and leaned back against the stone wall.

"A dragon will never allow a person on its back that it doesn't trust." Kieron twisted a piece of hay between his fingers as he thought about Vâken, his beloved dragon he had to leave behind in the caves. It took many times on Vâken's back to build that trust, but Kieron earned it and was grateful. He hoped he would see Vâken again. "And a person who can't ride a dragon will never have the chance to compete in the arena."

Thyler exhaled. "Whatever." He picked up a leather pouch full of oats and began feeding one of the dragons. After a while, Kieron thought he saw a slight grin on Thyler's face.

He left the boys alone to befriend the dragons. They were young dragons, still lithe and strong, with long, sinewy muscles twisting underneath their scaly skin. Their horns had not grown in fully, making it easy to saddle and ride them. But their wings were almost fully grown. The Wyverns moved clumsily as they continued to learn to walk with their large leathery wings, dragging along the ground for balance. Kieron chuckled as he watched them, knowing one day they would grow into those wings and be a formidable foe.

"They say he'll fight in the arena," said one boy.

"No, that can't be. He'll die! The King would never allow that," answered another boy.

"My father had said the King of Illiath is dead," Thyler said.

Kieron gasped and rushed over. "What?"

"It's true. My father said not long ago that King Alexander of Illiath died." Thyler set down the pouch.

"But how?" one boy asked.

"Not sure. Some say from a broken heart since Prince Peter was abducted." Thyler patted the dragon on its snout.

"I heard that the Prince was brought here to be trained to fight in the arena." Aerin backed into a dragon and it roared, sending him to the ground.

They know about Prince Peter, Kieron thought.. He glanced around, searching for crows inside the arena. *I must inform Dangler that he was right.*

The other boys laughed. Thyler reached out his hand to help him up. "You're a clutz, Aerin."

Aerin dusted off his trousers.

"How can that be?" Yon said. "Prince Peter is just a boy, like us. Those dragons are full grown monsters. They'll gobble him down whole."

"The Prince? In this horrible prison?" Kieron shook his head, pretending not to know anything about it. He tried to imagine what the Great Arena looked like, but couldn't. "What happens inside the Great Arena, anyway?"

Thyler squinted at him. "You don't know?"

"Men taken off the chains fight each other to the death," Yon said.

"And sometimes, Valbrand releases a few dragons to fight them, too. Just to make it interesting." Aerin chuckled.

"What about dragon riders?" Kealy asked.

"There are Dragon Games that happen inside the arena. Games of skill much like in here. Winners earn gold and another chance to ride. Losers fight on the ground like the others." Yon shook his head. "We've heard that men don't last long on the arena floor. Dragon riding is the way to go!"

"But Valbrand has the Prince fight on the arena floor?" Kieron looked over at Kealy.

"He must want him to be killed." She shrugged.

"But we hear in the mines that the boy they believe to be the prince is winning in the arena," Yon replied.

"How are things coming along?" Dangler asked. He removed his pocket watch from his vest and then glanced up. He noticed the long shadows outside the cave entrance. "It's getting late, way past noon."

"The stalls are cleaned, saddles are polished, and the dragons are fed." Kieron waved his hand over the progress of the day's work.

Dangler's eyebrows rose when he saw the boys befriending the dragons and, more importantly, the dragons warming up to the boys. His mouth dropped open.

"I'd say we've made excellent progress." Kieron rocked back and forth on his heels, proud of himself.

"I'll say." Dangler removed his cap and rubbed his head. "Well, let's get to work and see if these boys can ride."

But before they began, Kieron rushed over to Dangler to tell him what he'd heard.

"It is true, Dragon Master. These boys told us that the prince of Illiath is inside this prison," Kieron said to Dangler.

Dangler turned to face him. "What?" He turned to Kealy who nodded.

"We heard a rumor that the prince was abducted and brought to this prison to fight in the arena." Yon squinted. "Is it true?"

"I've not heard any such nonsense. Come on, let's get to work. Grab those saddles and bring them over here." Dangler waved his arm. When the boys moved away from them, Dangler turned to Kieron and Kealy. "How did they discover this about the prince?

Did you—"

"No," Kieron interrupted him. "They heard the rumor in the mines."

Dangler narrowed his eyes. "I will do my best to find out if Ethan is the prince. In the meantime, you must win a chance before Valbrand if you are to connect with Peter in the Great Arena and help him free these boys and you these dragons."

CHAPTER 5

With Kieron's face contorted, it was obvious to Dangler that Kieorn was sorely afraid.

"Don't let them see your fear." Dangler nodded to the other dragon rider across the dirt floor of the arena as he entered from the tunnel. "Your opponent; study his face. Take a look at those eyes."

"What?" Kieron shivered as he patted Fly's neck. He tried to ignore his fear.

"You're going to fly against him right now. I had planned on your contest to be tomorrow, but it must be now." Dangler nudged Kieron. "And you must win."

"Right now?" He swallowed as he noticed the intensity in the young man's eyes. "Does he think this is to the death?"

Dangler laughed. "He comes from the outside. One of Valbrand's recruits. He has won many tournaments, earning Valbrand much gold."

Kieron watched as Dangler strapped on the saddle to Fly's back. "Get up there, fly swiftly, hit that target and win. If you do, you'll earn a place before Valbrand."

"How much longer until this Ethan of Riverdale fights again?" Kieron asked.

"He remains forlorn after the death of the former knight who fought alongside him. Sir Nøel. But I'll see to it that Ethan fights very soon."

Kieron nodded that he understood Dangler. "Sir Nøel died?"

"I'll explain everything later. Now, get out there and win." Dangler used his cane and hobbled away. Kealy stood alongside the dragon stalls and Dangler found her. "He'll do well."

"Of course he will." She grinned.

Kieron managed to offer Kealy a weak smile.

"When he wins this contest, I will make sure he stands before Valbrand. This will ensure he fights in the Great Arena."

"But…" Kealy turned to Dangler. "He's not ready to fly in the arena yet. He'll need a few more practice runs."

"We don't have time for more practice runs." Dangler waved her off.

"He…Kieron isn't…he needs—"

"You said yourself that he's a good dragon rider." Dangler stared at her. "Is this true?"

Kealy swallowed. "I sure hope so. It's just that I thought we had more time." She glanced at the guards.

"There's not much time if Valbrand knows about the prince's plan to escape. Kieron will win a place before Valbrand; trust me."

A dragon's roar startled them both. In the center of the arena, Kieron and his opponent, both atop their dragons, faced one another. The umpire raised his arm and lowered it, causing the dragons to spread their leathery wings and take off in flight.

The boys cheered their friend on as he flew high above them.

Just think of flying back home between the trees in the White Forest, Kieron thought.

"Nothrien il aluein ish el," Kieron whispered to his dragon. "Fly well."

The dragon champed at the bit in its mouth and nodded in agreement with Kieron.

The prison guard with the horn raised it to his lips, preparing to start the tournament. Another guard appeared to make an announcement. "When the horn blasts, the tournament begins. The rider who places the most hens inside the wooden box over there wins. But you have only six minutes and if any chickens escape, they will not be counted unless you retrieve them and put them back into your box!"

"This will require swooping, quick maneuvering, and leaning over while staying in your saddle," Dangler said to the boys.

"If you fall off your dragon, you are disqualified," the announcer said.

"See? Listen to that?" Dangler pointed his finger at the judge.

"Do whatever it takes to stay on your dragon!" he shouted at the boys, staring at the two riders in the arena.

Kieron gripped the reins and steadied his dragon. *That's easy for Dangler to say. He's not on top of a dragon.*

The guard placed the horn to his lips and blew the horn, causing Kieron, his opponent, and their dragons to take flight. Dirt and pebbles flew through the air as the dragons flapped their wings.

Another prison guard released the chickens, and chaos ensued. Kieron turned his dragon and dove toward the chickens. He leaned over, holding onto the horn of the saddle, squeezed his thighs to hold onto the dragon, and scooped up two chickens.

"Yes!" he shouted. "Whoa!" He swerved his dragon out of the way of the other rider, who swiped a chicken out of Kieron's arms as he passed by.

"Hey!" Kieron frowned. Now he understood how the competition would work. He'd get the chickens and his opponent would steal them. As Kieron flew above the action, he heard Kealy shout, "Watch out! He'll swipe the chickens from your arms. Get them into the box right after you grab them!"

"No kidding." Kieron frowned, turned his dragon, and dove down.

Kieron heeled the ribs of his dragon and dropped the one chicken into the box. His opponent had two of them inside already.

I'll need about twenty more in order to win.

The opponent swooped down and attempted to grab the frightened chickens as they ran all over the dirt arena. The dust filled the air.

Kieron turned his dragon and nudged him to fly faster. He leaned over again, his shoulder almost scraping the ground, and grabbed two chickens.

"Get over to the box!" Kieron ordered his dragon. He tossed the two chickens into the box and swerved to the right. Flapping its wings, Fly took off toward more chickens, almost colliding with the opponent on his dragon. "Look out!"

His opponent maneuvered his dragon out of the way just in time. Kieron flew to the box and tossed in three chickens.

"Yes!" Kieron shouted. Hovering above the arena for a few seconds, he could see the other rider struggling to stay in his saddle and grab chickens at the same time. *I have an advantage.* He smiled.

"Kieron!" Thyler shouted. "We only need three more!"

"So do I," said the competitor.

Only five chickens remained on the arena floor.

Nudging his dragon, Kieron and Fly flew low to the ground, ready to swoop up three more chickens. Yon and Aerin followed alongside the arena.

The race to the finish began as the dragons focused their eyes on the prize.

A chance at freedom.

The competitor's dragon sped up and the rider leaned over in his saddle, but instead of scooping up the chickens, he scooped up a handful of dirt and threw it into the face of Kieron's dragon, causing Fly to pull up, squawk, and shake its head.

"No!" Kieron grabbed Fly's neck to keep from falling off.

The dragon blinked, trying to get the dirt from its eyes.

"Eleon, is thriel ileon!" Kieron shouted. "You'll have to fly blind. Listen to my voice, trust me!"

The competitor scooped up two chickens, but Kieron was able to smack one out of his arms and grab it before it hit the ground.

The prison boys cheered and rushed to the sidelines. But right before Kieron hopped off his dragon to celebrate the victory, the horn blew.

"Now for round two," the announcer said.

"Round two?" Yon asked. "I thought this was it. What gives?"

Kieron thought about it. "I thought there was only one round as well."

Yon handed Kieron a damp rag to wipe the dirt out of his eyes. Kieron also helped his dragon by wiping her eyes. "Better?" he asked her. Fly squawked. "Good because we've more flying to do."

Two large brass rings were brought out as well as three targets.

"In this round, the winning team must successfully shoot the arrows through all three rings, hitting the bullseye on all three targets." The announcer pointed to the rings. "While the rings are moving."

"Team?" Kieron asked.

Kealy made her way over to him, leading her dragon by the reins. "We're ready to go."

"One more victory and you'll have your place before Valbrand. And then you can speak your language to the big dragons of the arena." Dangler patted Kieron's shoulder.

"Dragon speak." Kieron thought about it. He studied the dragons of his opponents. *If I can speak to those dragons about the plan, the maybe they'll help us to win.*

The prison guards attached the rings to chains dangling from the rock ceiling, and tapped the rings to make them swing back and forth.

"While they're moving?" Aerin whined. "That'll be impossible."

Kieron's heart sank at the thought of the complex challenge, but when he compared it to being stuck in the mountain prison for the rest of his life, he knew he had to win the round.

"I can do it." Kealy winked.

"I know you can," Kieron said. "But can I?"

Kealy mounted her dragon. "I have every confidence in you."

"But you can't. You can't get your arrows through those targets while riding your dragons." Thyler jerked his hand at the moving targets.. "It's almost impossible to accomplish that. They're setting you up for failure."

"Doesn't matter. Only one of us has to win, remember?" Kieron took the leather gloves Dangler had provided him. He walked over to the rows of quivers filled with arrows and selected one. His competitor selected a quiver, too.

Remembering what Aislinn had always taught him about good sportsmanship, Kieron walked over to his opponent and held out his hand. "Good luck."

But the boy ignored him and went back to his waiting dragon.

"Seems you two have a lot in common," Thyler said. "You're both arrogant."

"I know." Kieron chortled and attached the quiver to the saddle. "It's okay. I've been doing archery all my life." He pictured his older brother helping him hold the bow while his sister, Aislinn, set up the target for practice. His eyes stung with tears as he remembered his family. *This is for you, Théan and Aislinn.*

"Riders to your marks," the announcers said.

"Good luck, Kieron." Yon shook his hand. "You can do it."

The other boys patted Kealy on her back. "Ride well!" they shouted to her.

Thyler approached. "Aim true." He shook Kieron's hand.

"Always," Kieron said.

∽

Kieron gripped the reins in his hands tightly as he sat in the saddle atop Fly. The pressure of not knowing how to do archery proficiently, especially from a dragon's back, began to overtake him. He wiped the sweat from his brow before it dripped into his eyes, stinging them and affecting his vision. He'd need keen vision for this round, that was for sure.

Having never inspected the arrows in the quiver he selected, he turned and started to remove one, but the guard pointed at him and scowled.

"No pre-loading your bows!" he shouted.

Kieron let his quiver go.

The announcer placed the horn to his lips.

"Kieron! Turn around!" Kealy shouted.

"Get ready!" Thyler interjected.

He nodded and grinned at Kieron.

Aerin put his hands together and waved them in the air as a victory salute.

"You can do this!" Aerin cheered. But his wide smile slowly turned into a frown.

Three more opponents entered the arena atop young Draco dragons.

"What's this?" Kealy asked. She searched the area for Dangler, but he was nowhere to be found.

"That's not fair, six to two." Thyler scowled.

Kealy inspected the opponents and Kieron. "We'll need more help. Come on!"

She took hold of Thyler's arm and led him to where the dragons rested. "Grab one and let's go!"

"Wait...what?" Thyler glanced around.

Kealy saddled a unsuspecting dragon and placed the bridle over its snout. "Grab a saddle and let's go!" she ordered Yon and Thyler.

"Wait!" Kealy's shout came from behind Kieron. "There's more riders for this round!"

The guards jerked their heads around to see what was happening.

"What are you doing?" Kieron asked his friends as they approached atop their dragons.

"We're competing to make it fair." Kealy gripped the reins of Thyler and Yon's dragons and adjusted the bow over her shoulder.

"Fair?" Kieron looked over at Thyler. "But you said you've never competed in archery before." Kieron raised his eyebrows.

"Shhh." Thyler nodded toward the competitors. "They don't know that."

"Riders ready?" the guard shouted.

"No!" Thyler struggled to take hold of the reins and mount his dragon. But it was too late.

The horn sounded and the riders took to flight, zipping around each other like angry bees after the same flower. Except Kieron knew his friends desired more than victory or a trophy in the Dragon Games. They wanted a freedom.

He removed an arrow with one hand and gripped the bow with the other, squeezing his thighs together so as not to fall off the saddle. His dragon, Fly, raced toward the first target, and Kieron loaded his bow with the arrow, taking note of the speed with which the brass ring swung back and forth before the target. He stretched the bow string back as his dragon raced forward. Just then, a competitor's dragon swerved directly in front of Kieron, blocking his view. He released the arrow but pointed it upwards to keep from hitting the boy atop the dragon. But the boy shot his arrow and hit the target.

Kieron swung Fly around to try again at the other target.

"He didn't get the bullseye, Kieron!" Yon shouted from his dragon.

Good. Kieron knew he still had a chance. This time he would not fail.

He loaded the bow once again and nudged his dragon. "Uth vas, bethiel el ién!" he shouted. Kieron knew Fly would have to glance left and right for the approaching competition because he couldn't. He'd have to keep his eye on the target and the brass ring swinging back and forth, taunting him like a pesky clock. Time was running out. Kieron and his team needed to get before the warden and fast.

He loaded his bow with another arrow. There were four left to hit all three targets, or else. Kieron stretched the bow string back across his chest, being sure to squeeze his thighs even tighter, because at any moment, Fly would have to swerve out of the way or even spin around to best the competition coming toward them.

The target was straight ahead and the brass ring swung left, leaving the target wide open for a split second. With his left eye closed, Kieron knew he couldn't see if the competitor was flying in from that side. All he could do was hope Fly knew.

Right before he released the arrow, Fly spun upside down to fool the fast approaching dragon on the left, but Kieron never took his eye off the target. Even after being upside down for a second, he released the arrow as they spun back upright in time to see it hit the bullseye.

The crowd of boys cheered him. Fly swooped up right before crashing into the target. "Whoa!" Kieron shouted as they flew straight up to the ceiling, then hovered there for a second before free-falling down again.

Kieron loaded another arrow as Fly made a pass by the other targets. But before he could shoot, the crowd of prisoners cheered. Kieron jerked his head around and saw one of the competitors celebrating having made a bullseye.

Fly snorted her disapproval. "Don't worry," Kieron said. "We have another chance. Let's go!"

Kealy flew her dragon low to the ground, gathering speed with each beat of his wings. "My turn." She loaded her bow, took aim, and released the arrow.

"Come on, come on," Kieron muttered as he watched Kealy's arrow fly through the air, through the ring, and hit the target. "Yes!"

Kealy and her dragon spun around and raced over the cheering boys.

Kieron squinted at a target and loaded his bow. "Come on, Fly." He nudged her. Together, they swiped the ground. Dirt and pebbles flew into the air and Fly's belly scraped the floor of the arena. Kieron pulled the string back and took aim at the target as they sped toward it. Fly squawked to alert him to the dragon flying toward them on the left again. This time, Kieron smiled confidently. Aislinn had taught him how to aim while flying fast and with both eyes on the target. But would he remember how to get it done?

"Pull the string back, open your chest wide, never take your eyes of that target!" she'd command.

Kieron took aim and released the arrow. It barely missed the brass ring as it swung right.

Fly swooped up and back down again.

"Yes!" Yon shouted. "Go, Kieron!"

"You can do it!" shouted Aerin.

Thyler flew his dragon over to where Kieron was. "I want to try!" he shouted.

Kicron's eyebrows rose. "Are you sure?"

Thyler turned his dragon, loaded his bow, and took aim.

As an opponent raced over to beat him to the target, both Yon and Kealy flew their dragons nearby to cause a distraction.

Kieron watched and wondered. "Uthriel vas ileon!" he shouted.

To his amazement, all the dragons turned their heads to Kieron except Thyler's dragon. Without stopping, Thyler and his dragon sped toward the remaining target.

The oppents sat atop stunned dragons and desperately nudged them to fly. But they hovered and stared bewilderedly at Kieron.

It worked, he thought. *They understood me.*

Thyler released his arrow and it flew toward the target, striking it dead on.

The boys cheered and the horn sounded.

The game was tied.

Each rider had one chance left and not much time.

The prison guard pushed the brass ring in front of the last target so it swung back and forth.

A rush of heat flowed through Kieron's body. He pulled on Fly's reins and the dragon beat its leathery wings. *We've got this.* Together, they dove to the target, unabated since all the other dragons hovered and watched, while their riders seethed in anger and frustration.

But blood splattered into Kieron's eyes.

"What's this?" He reached up and wiped his face. "Where's this coming from?"

"Oh no." Thyler and his dragon flew by. Kieron could see the worried look on his face. "Your dragon is injured."

"What's going on?" Kealy shouted to them as she approached.

"My dragon is injured?" Kieron held back his dragon and searched its wings. "Where?"

"There!" Thyler pointed to an arrow in Fly's underbelly.

Kieron threw his head back. "No! This can't be happening."

"I'll shoot this next target." Kealy and her dragon flew to the arena floor where she loaded her bow and shot an arrow at the target, buying Kieron some time.

"What do you want to do?" Thyler asked Kieron.

Fly yanked on the reins, insisting on returning to the games, but Kieron kept the dragon back. "No, you're injured!"

It was no use. The lithe dragon took over and flew down to the arena floor, while Kieron searched the opponents. "Which one of you shot her?"

But they all grinned wickedly.

Kealy shot her arrow but it missed.

Fly flapped her wings and raced toward the loan target. Kieron leered at his opponents, still atop their hovering dragons. He loaded his bow and his eyebrows rose. "Oh no," he said. He hadn't noticed the worn tip on the arrowhead. It was dull. Kieron knew it may not stick.

"Al iniâl us il ish nierienthal," Kieron told his dragon. "We cannot rely on the sharpness of the arrow, so we're going to have to rely on your speed and strength. Can you do it? Nierienthal?"

The dragon snorted so Kieron loaded the bow and stretched the bow string back. A competitor, hovering nearby, did the same.

Kieron heeled Fly's ribs and sent her speeding toward the target. The competitor shot his arrow at Fly. The dragon spun around over and over, but Kieron stayed on the saddle by squeezing his thighs and digging his heels into Fly's sides. The dragon roared, not from pain, but from excitement.

"Look at Kieron go!" Aerin shouted.

They all watched him go.

The competitor's arrow couldn't match Fly's speed. Fly made it to the target first, giving Kieron enough time to stretch the bow string back even further. The string began to cut into his fingers, but he had to hold on for a few more seconds. Kieron screamed from the pain and excitement.

"I can't watch." Thyler covered his eyes.

"Look!" Kealy shouted.

Kieron released the arrow as Fly swerved left, almost colliding with another dragon. It swerved right and away from the target. The competitor's arrow missed Fly, striking the cave wall.

But Kieron's arrow struck the target and even with the dull arrow tip, it sunk deep into the bullseye.

The crowd remained silent as they saw the arrow jiggle. If it fell out, they'd lose. There would be no winner heading to the Great Arena to represent the prison riders.

Kieron tugged on the reins to turn Fly. They flew back around to see the arrow. The prison guard and announcer stood in front of the target, watching the arrow.

Kieron landed Fly in the center of the arena and waited.

The announcer turned with a scowl on his face. Kieron frowned.

But then the scowl on the announcer's face slowly turned into wha many would consider a grin.

"The arrow remains in the target," he shouted.

The boys on the sideline cheered and ran toward Kieron. "You did it! You did it!" Yon shouted.

But Kieron couldn't celebrate until the announcement was made. He watched the announcer make his way over to him and Fly. He took Kieron's arm and raised it high.

"We have our winner!"

Kieron tilted his head back and shouted with joy while all his friends patted his back and Fly's neck.

They yanked him off his dragon, but Kieron fell to the ground. His thighs had cramped up from squeezing his dragons so tightly.

"Ouch!" he cried and rubbed his legs.

"Are you alright?" Kealy asked.

"I'm fine!" Kieron laughed. "Get help for Fly."

Thyler's dragon landed nearby. He hopped off and ran over to Kieron and Fly, waving for a boy to bring them a rag. They pressed it onto Fly's open wound. But it was no use. The beast fell over onto its side, breathing heavily.

"No! Hang in there, Fly!" Kieron cried, pressing onto the wound even harder as the blood flowed onto the dirt. "We've got to get the arrow out!"

Kieron stroked the dragon's chest as it heaved in and out. "You'll be alright."

Kealy covered her mouth and tears filled her eyes. The arena grew still and silent.

"Hold on," Kieron whispered. "Stay with me. Mythri il ien." In his mind, he saw Aislinn's face. *It's my fault. I caused this. Don't leave me.*

But Fly's eyes slowly closed and she breathed her last.

"No!" Kieron buried his head onto the dragon's side and wept.

"Not again."

Thyler and the others watched in silence for a moment.

"You did it, Fly." Kieron whispered to the dead dragon. "You won this contest. I'm so sorry I failed you, Aislinn."

"Aislinn?" Yon whispered to Kealy.

She shook her head and put a finger to her lips.

Kieron continued to stroke the dead dragon's side.

"This is all so tragic." Kealy sniffled.

Kieron wiped his eyes and stood. The arena grew silent and still. He sighed and thanked the little dragon. "El, elién."

"Come on," Thyler motioned for the others to help him with his and Kealy's dragon. "Let's get them some water."

Dangler hobbled over to Kieron, who used his sleeve to wipe the tears and dirt from his face. "What's this?" Dangler asked. He pointed to Fly's side where the arrow protruded and blood dripped from between her scales.

"She's dead," Kieron whispered.

Dangler walked over to a small box he had placed within a crevice of the cave wall. He brought over the box and showed Kieron what was inside. "Do you recognize this, boy?"

Kieron shook his head.

"Uthriel. It's a special powder made from ground dragon horns. We use to make the healing paste." Dangler took some of the fine powder into his fingers.

"Uthriel. A healing paste?" Kieron tilted his head.

"That's right. An elf gave this to me years ago. I tend to use it on injured riders, but once in a while, a dragon will need it."

"It can heal?" Kieron shook his head. "I don't think it can bring a dead dragon back to life."

Dangler didn't budge.

"Can it?" Kieron ran to a rain barrel and retrieved some water. He mixed the powder with the water to create a paste. It had a unique smell that repelled the other dragons. They snorted and returned to their stalls.

Kieron rubbed the paste into the wound and waited.

"Rub it in good." Dangler pointed to the wound.

Kieron obeyed.

Remove the arrow," Dangler ordered.

With Kealy's help, Kieron gently removed the arrow. It slid out easily.

"Rub more paste onto the wound. If this works, it should heal quickly."

"If it works?" Kealy asked.

Dangler shrugged.

Kieron rubbed the paste in deeper, reaching over and stroking Fly's neck. *Please,* he thought. *Please come back.*

Thyler and the others carefully approached the scene.

"Ishniel, mythrion, il ish. Uthre vas," he whispered to the dragon, rubbing its snout. "Uthre vas. Come back, Fly. You're a champion. You did it. You won. Please come back."

Yon sighed. "I don't know. It's been dead for too long."

Thyler shook his head.

"Come on, Fly," Kealy whispered. "You can do it. You're a champion. You can—"

"Look at that!" Yon shouted.

Fly opened her eyes and blinked a few times.

Kieron fell back and gasped at the sight.

"The dragon's alive again!" Yon turned to the others.

Kealy hopped up and down. "It worked!"

Kieron turned to Dangler, who smiled. "I wasn't sure if it would work, but it did."

Thyler picked up the box of dragon powder. "Who knew ground dragon horns could heal this way?"

Dangler took the box from Thyler. "I'll take that."

Fly's tail thumped on the ground as her sides went in and out with each breath. Kieron hugged Fly's neck. "Thank you, friend."

CHAPTER 6

D angler set down some food onto the table for Kieron to eat. "I don't think she should fly in the games."

Kieron shoved his plate of food away and stood up. "What? What do you mean?"

"Look at her." Dangler pointed to Fly, lying on the ground in the cage. "The dragon's exhausted, and the next games inside the Great Arena are just two days away." Dangler folded his arms.

"Fly needs to rest," Kealy agreed.

"But what dragon will I ride? I won't have enough time to train it and speak with it. I tell you, it won't work!" Kieron shoved his chair to the ground. "We don't have time. We need to free these dragons now!"

"Hey!" Dangler bent over to retrieve it. "Watch my furniture."

"Sorry." Kieron frowned. Not having a dragon he could trust would take away his advantage. His mind raced and he became dizzy. "What am I going to do?" Kieron rubbed his tense forehead. "I'll never win the tournament now."

"Excuse me, elf, but I think you've forgotten our mission. You're not flying in the arena to win. You're flying in the arena to speak to the dragons and explain the plan to them. My mind's made up. This dragon needs to rest."

"You're right." Kieron pulled the chair over to the table. "I suppose I did forget the plan for a moment."

Dangler chuckled. "Well, I suppose you could ride *this* dragon." Dangler waved for one of his handlers to bring in a dragon.

Kieron shook his head. "No, it's no use. I won't have enough time to bond and teach the dragon how to—"

The dragon squawked as the handler lead him in. When Kieron

heard it, he slowly turned around.

"It can't be!" He ran over to his friend, Vâken. "It can't be! I left you inside that cave!" He embraced his dragon's neck and almost knocked the beast over.

Vâken nodded and nuzzled his head on Kieron's chest. With hope in his eyes, Kieron gripped tightly to his old friend.

"So, I think you'll have plenty of success riding this dragon." Dangler laughed.

"But...how? When?" Kealy asked.

"The Riders found him flying around the prison entrance. They captured it and ordered me to hold it in one of my cells for training. I gladly obliged. When I did so, the creature dragged me over to this arena. That's when I knew. I had a feeling it knew who you were."

"Oh Vâken." Kieron grinned. "Now we'll win a chance to free all the dragons."

Kieron took a sponge and loaded it with cool water. He wiped down Fly's back and sides as she ate some fish. Her tail swished back and forth in the stall. Next, he watched as Vâken enjoyed his fish.

"So we have a winner." Dangler watched as Kieron and Kealy cared for the dragons.

Kieron nodded. "Do you think we captured the attention of Valbrand?"

"We shall see. And if you did, you'll have the chance to select three for your team to accompany you."

"I select Kealy and Thyler for sure." Kieron squinted as he thought of a third teammate to select. "I suppose Yon can join in."

"Alright now." Dangler slapped his thigh. "You need to eat and rest up for more training with your dragon. Come now, let's return to my living quarters."

Kieron nodded in agreement, walked Vâken and Fly to their stalls, and said goodnight to his dragons.

"You've been through a lot," Dangler said. "But don't worry. It'll all be over with soon, and you can return home."

Home.

"Vâken"

The very idea of it made a knot in Kieron's throat that made it hard to swallow and breathe. He wasn't sure he could ever go home again now. Thèan must have given up and returned home to tell their father about Kieron's whereabouts. His father's angry face appeared in his mind, making Kieron wince. Could he ever go back to the farm and the way things were before?

As they walked through the hall, boys who were prisoners dumped large buckets of coal they had mined into even larger bins, one after the other. Kieron noticed their eyes were vacant, without a trace of hope of ever being rescued. Staying in the prison would be a punishment worse than death, but returning to the farm gave Kieron almost as much reservation.

Facing his father's wrath again was more than he could bear. No, Kieron knew he could probably never go home. He'd have to start again near the pond, his favorite fishing hole, with his dragons and not much else. But he could do it. *Father taught me how to plant and harvest. Thèan taught me how to protect myself. Aislinn and Mother taught me how to make a home.* He sighed. *I guess I am on my own now.*

∽

"I'll prepare you some food. Then you'll get some rest." Dangler opened the door to his home.

"Surprise!" shouted the boys on Kieron's team. "Hail the conquering hero!" Yon, Thyler, Aerin, and the other boys raised their arms high above their heads.

They rushed to the door and grabbed Kieron by his shoulders, almost knocking him over.

"Congratulations!" Aerin shouted. "I thought I had seen the best, but you both are definitely the best dragon riders ever!"
Kieron shook his head. "No, you should see my brother. He is the best."

Dangler leaned in to whisper in Kieron's ear. "Let them shower you with praise. It'll make them happy."

Kieron understood. And for the night, he and Kealy allowed their new friends to brag and give them the praise Kieron didn't think he had earned. The smiles on their faces and the joy in their laughter was all that mattered. He had given them something to smile about. He had given them joy they hadn't had in a long time.

"Here's to Kealy and Thyler and their part in the competition." Kieron raised his cup of apple cider. "And to you all, cheering us on. We could hear you from afar and it really helped to keep us going."

The boys cheered again and patted Kealy and Thyler on their backs.

"Not bad for a girl elf," Thyler mocked.

Kealy smirked at him. "Ha ha. Very funny."

Dangler placed the food he had prepared onto the table and the boys quickly gathered around and picked up their knives and forks to eat the roasted chicken with potatoes.

Yon tied his linen napkin around his neck. "Are these the chickens from the tournament?" he asked.

Everyone laughed, including Kieron.

After dinner, the boys fell asleep in a tiny room with a wood burning stove to keep them warm. No sleep came to Kieron, though. He lay on the bed, atop a straw mattress, sweating bullets on the cold night. Over and over again in his mind he played out every last detail of the archery portion of the tournament. His brother, who last participated in the the Dragon Games two autumns earlier, had instructed Kieron on what to do and what not to do.

"Don't approach too quickly," he had told him. "Trust your dragon. Vâken knows what to do."

Kieron raised his head and spotted his faithful dragon curled up by the boys, snoring away. He envied how peacefully the dragon slept, without a care in the world. Vâken was a fierce competitor when it came to dragon riding. If they won in the Great Arena, then they could prove themselves before Prince Thætil and perhaps win a place on the Queen's Dragon Riders. The thought brought a wide grin to his face. *No!* Kieron shook the thought out of his head. *That's not the plan. Our mission is to earn a chance to fly with the other dragons. I'll speak to them and convince them to help us escape. Yes, that's the plan.*

Kieron stared above. The dancing shadows on the ceiling of the room carved out of the mountain entertained his thoughts for a moment. But then thoughts of home returned. A single tear formed in the corner of one eye, but he quickly wiped it away. *I cannot allow my fear and emotions to get the best of me. I have a clear task at hand, and I cannot concentrate on anything else.* Kieron smiled because he was finally thinking like Aislinn.

The door of the room creaked open, jarring Kieron. He sat up and saw Dangler motioning for him to come into the hall. Whipping the blanket off his legs, Kieron tip-toed over the boys, Kealy, and Vâken to meet with Dangler in the hallway.

"What?" he whispered.

"Come this way." Danlger led him to the table, cleared of all the dishes and cups.

"What is it?" Kieron asked.

Dangler ambled over to the fire in the pit where he cooked his meals. He stoked the fire with an iron rod. "The warden sees an opportunity to win gold coins by having you fight in the arena."

"We can fight in the arena?"

"This is why I woke you. Valbrand has asked to see you tomorrow."

"Tomorrow?" Kieron's eyes grew wide.

"Yes. The plan is now set in motion. You and your team will fly in the arena as a distraction. You will have the chance to speak to the dragons, gain their trust, and ask them to help us free all the dragons and slaves inside this prison." Dangler gestured with the fire poker.

"What about Valbrand?" Kieron's eyes filled with worry.

Dangler shrugged. "Valbrand might be suspicious, but I suspect he could care less, as long as your team wins and he has his gold." Dangler shook his head. "The warden is impressed by your skill and will command that you fly dragons in the arena."

"I understand."

Dangler nodded. "Yes. The dragons are larger, more fierce, and hungrier. The risk is higher, but if you can speak to them and gain their trust…"

"And stay alive." Kieron swallowed the fear down but it got stuck in his throat like a chicken bone. "Sure. No problem."

Larger dragons? His mind went to the angry female dragon captured in the forest. Her size and strength were unlike anything Kieron had seen before. *More fierce and hungry?* He shivered. But she did trust him in the end. She trusted him enough to allow him and Kealy to land their dragons in her cave. Kieron squinted as he thought about it.

"Don't worry." Dangler searched the area for crows. "We have an ally. A most excellent ally."

Intrigued, Kieron leaned in close to hear.

"Remember, Ethan of Riverdale told me that he once met the Dragon of the Forest." Dangler's eyes twinkled.

Kieron leaned back and his jaw dropped. "And you believe him?"

"I do." The corners of Dangler's mouth rose into a hopeful grin. "I do believe he's the one."

"Prince Peter?" Kieron asked. "But why is he hiding his identity? If Valbrand knows that the prince is inside this prison, why hasn't he ordered that Peter be killed?"

Dangler hobbled over to Kieron and leaned in close. Kieron could see specks of blue in Dangler's green eyes. "Because he wins in the arena!" He nodded. "He and that former knight make Valbrand rich."

"But Lord Bedlam…" Kieron squinted as he tried to understand.

Dangler placed his finger to his lips. "Shhh. Remember the spies."

Kieron glanced around the room.

"Rumor has it that Bedlam ordered the abduction of the prince by the Riders of Rünbrior."

"So he wants the prince held captive in here." Kieron stood and paced the room. "If King Alexander is dead and this Ethan of Riverdale is the prince. Then who rules Illiath?"

Dangler shook his head. "Who knows. All I know is that if Ethan is the prince and he has met the Dragon of the Forest, then the Great beast will come help us."

The legends of old said no one man had ever entered the Dragon Forest and lived, yet Prince Peter once met the Great Dragon of Promise. Kieron sat back down. "I remember hearing about the war with Lord Caragon and how Prince Peter rode the Dragon of the Forest. And how the evil Lord Caragon's men fought to kill the Dragon for its impenetrable scales. Is that true or legend?"

"True." Dangler grinned once again. "Prince Peter is the one."

"The chosen one to finally bring the long-awaited end to the Darkness and Lord Bedlam once and for all?" Kieron stared at the dancing flames of the firepit. "Wow."

The Dragon of Promise.

According to Elfin legend, a dragon was promised to heal the land and bring all dragons and men together in peace. Elves already made peace with the dragons, but men abused them and created a gulf between themselves and the beasts. But many wizards had told kings of old that a dragon would be hatched that would finally bridge that gulf to bring lasting healing to the land forever. The Dragon of the Forest was that Dragon of Promise. Hatched and raised by elves long ago, the dragon challenged the rogue dragons and their leader, the Black Dragon, to join with it and live in peace. But the Black Dragon and its minions wanted to war instead. Their hatred toward men was too great.

So, the elves, men, and the Dragon of Promise went to war. The Black Dragon was exiled to the Ranvieg Mountains and the Dragon went to live peacefully inside the Dragon Forest, where no man dared to enter without permission.

Peter had that permission.

Kieron shook his head in disbelief. "I have heard the tales of the battle of Illiath where the Dragon of the Forest gave up its scales to save the kingdom. I always thought it was just a legend."

"It is true. Prince Peter rode the beast's back and fought off Lord Caragon." Dangler winked. "And that's why I know he's the one. That's why I gave him my book."

Confused, Kieron cocked his head. "What book?"

"The Dragon Chronicles," he replied. "All Dragon Masters of the past have chronicled all we know about dragons and put this knowledge into one book. Ethan of Riverdale is studying it now to learn more about dragons."."

Kieron's eyebrows rose. "I've always wanted to write such a book!"

"It's already done." Dangler pretended to write something in the air. "I placed all my knowledge about dragons in that book."

Kieron shook his head. "But if the Dragon of the Forest perished like everyone says, he can no longer help any of us."

Dangler chuckled. "That's the myth...the legend."

"But what if it's truth?"

"We can hope. . But it's time for you to go back to bed. I'll take this." He picked up his crane and hobbled to the door. "Tell no one what you have heard me say, understand?"

"Bed? Sleep?" Kieron's face crinkled up. "How can I sleep now?

If the Great Dragon lives and Prince Peter is here inside this prison, and a plan is set in motion to free all the dragons and slaves...This is all too exciting. I cannot possibly—"

"Listen, you have to stand before Valbrand in the morning. He's the man who has the power to keep you imprisoned here forever if you don't impress him tomorrow. And if he's bored with you, he has the power to feed you to his personal dragon, Scythar." Dangler crossed his arms. "So, get some rest." He scooted Kieron toward the door. "We've a big day tomorrow."

Kieron nodded and return to bed. But his head was swimming with all sorts of scenarios. Prince Peter fighting dragons in the arena, the Dragon of the Forest alive and protecting the kingdom again, the Dragon Chronicles book...all these images took over his mind.

As he made his way back into the bed, he wished he could tell all his friends what he had just learned, but he knew he couldn't.

Not yet.

Inside his heart, Kieron was glad that a plan to free all the dragons and prisoners was in the making, but he was extremely relieved that he wasn't the only one tasked with seeing the plan through.

He pulled the blanket up to his chin. His task was to fly Vâken inside the Great Arena, speak to the other dragons, gain their trust, and stay alive.

Stay alive.

With giant dragons chasing him, it would be far more intense than the Dragon Games could ever be. But the horrific abductions of dragons and maiming them to fight inside the arena to the death revealed the *real* dragon games and how evil they really were. The thought of how Valbrand and his Riders of Rünbrior kidnap so many children after trying out for the Dragon Games only to be captured and imprisoned made his stomach burn inside Kieron's body.

"Kieron," Thyler whispered..

"Yes?"

"Where were you?" Thyler raised up onto his elbow.

"I couldn't sleep, so I spoke with Dangler for a moment."

"Ah, I see."

"Why aren't you asleep?"

Thyler shrugged. "Thinking of home."

Kieron sat up. "Really?"

"It's been a while since I've been home." Thyler stared at the fireglow of the wood stove.

"Tell me about your home." Kieron pulled his legs close and rested his chin on his knees.

"I'm from Heinland's Gate."

Kieron nodded. "I know that land. That's near the east shore."

"A long way from here, I know." Thyler sighed. "I have four older brothers."

"Four?" Kieron's eyes widened. "I have one. I can't imaging having four."

Thyler chuckled. "They are all with the Queen's Dragon Riders."

"*All* of them?" Kieron scooted closer to Thyler. "That's incredible."

He nodded. "Yes. They have made my father so proud."

Kieron nudged him. "You will make your father proud, too."

His eyes grew shiny. "I don't think so. I can't compare to my brothers. You saw me try in the smaller arena."

"You did your best."

"I'm no dragon rider." Thyler sniffled.

"Heinland's Gate, huh?" Kieron asked. "I know the meadow there."

"That's where the first Dragon Games were held."

"Yes!" Kieron straightened. "I thought so. That's a very famous tilting field."

"What are you two talking about?" Kealy asked from the darkness.

"Shhh. Go back to sleep." Kieron put his finger to his mouth.

"I also have three sisters." Thyler wiggled his toes. "They made me these socks."

Kieron smiled. But when he realized he had nothing of his sister, Aislinn, he frowned.

"What's the matter?" Thyler asked.

Kieron shook his head. "Nothing. It's just that you're lucky that you have something to remember your sisters by. I don't have anything."

"Home…" Thyler lay back down and placed his hands behind his head. "I hope to see it again one day."

Kieron scooted over to his own bed roll. "Yes. Together, we'll complete our mission and free the dragons and slaves inside this prison so we all can go home again."

"If we stay alive." Thyler rolled over. "Good night, Kieron. You flew well today. You are already a dragon rider to me."

Kieron grinned. "Thank you, Thyler."

Returning home again. Kieron wanted to make sure Thyler, Yon, Aerin, and Kealy all made it back to their villages. But home was no longer for him. *Don't think about that now. Think about the task at hand.* Kieron rolled over. *You will stand before Valbrand in the morning. You have to impress him to allow you to fly in the arena. That's the plan. Stick to it, Kieron.* He made a fist with his hand. *No fear. No doubt. You can do this.*

Finally, Kieron closed his eyes and fell fast asleep.

CHAPTER 7

Kieron shook Thyler awake. "Come on. It's time for breakfast."

"Breakfast!" Thyler leapt up and headed toward the door, hopping over Yon, Kealy, and the other boys.

"Ouch!" Yon rubbed his head. "You kicked me."

"Food!" Thyler waved the boys to the door and they all ran after him. Some kicked Kieron's dragon on accident.

Vâken growled, and a silvery stream of smoke rose from its nostrils.

"Steady, boy," Kieron said as he stroked its head. "You all would be wise to remember that my dragon hasn't had his fire glands removed."

Yon's eyebrows rose. "Good to know."

Vâken's eyes narrowed to slits and the corners of his mouth rose into a slight grin.

Kealy stood and stretched her back. "Ugh. Sleeping on the cold ground is not good for sore muscles." She scratched her head and tried to undo her tangled white hair. "This is not good."

In the main area of Dangler's home, he stood with his arms crossed over his wide chest. "No time for food."

The boys slid to a stop and groaned their displeasure.

"What? Why not?" Thyler asked with a frown.

Dangler stretched out his arm and pointed to Kealy, Kieron, and Thyler. "Because all of you are due to stand before Valbrand today. Right now! Let's go!"

Kealy spat on her hands and smoothed out her tangled hair. Kieron straightened out his tunic.

"But I'm starving!" Thyler grumbled.

"Can't we have time to freshen up a bit?" Kealy asked.

Dangler scowled at them. "What? Listen, we only have so much time. The plan is in motion and we have to execute it immediately."

Kealy grimaced and placed her hands on her hips. "Then you should have woken us earlier. I say, let's eat."

"Yes!" Thyler rushed to the table and filled his plate with food as the other boys joined in.

Kealy made her way to a wash basin in the corner, filled it with water from a nearby jug, and washed her face.

Kieron nodded. "Dangler's right. We have to go now. We don't want to anger Valbrand." He shuffled his way past Kealy and the others and stood next to an impatient Dangler. Thyler and the boys guzzled down apple juice and biscuits as fast as they could.

Kealy made her way to the door. "Fine." She quickly braided her hair. "I suppose we will eat later…in our own homes, when we are reunited with our families."

"Yes!" Yon cried. He led a cheer for the three as they departed into the darkened hallway. He lifted his cup of juice. "Good luck!"

"You there." Danlger squinted at Yon and the others. "Clean up this mess when you are finished and get those dragons fed. Understand?"

Yon gulped and slowly lowered his cup. "Aye, sir."

Kieron, Kealy, and Thyler walked down the scarcely lit corridor, following Dangler as he hobbled along.

"What do we do when we get there?" whispered Kieron.

Kealy shrugged. "We'll do what we're told."

"That's right!" Dangler replied.

Kieron and Kealy kept quiet the rest of the way to where Valbrand's living quarters were. The musty smell of soot mixed with mildew made Kieron's nose crinkle. He noticed the only light in the carved hallways were the torches, hanging in sconces made of twisted metal strips lining the walls. The dancing flames alerted him to air seeping in from the outside world. Would he ever see the outside world again? The meadows adorned with purple flowers at the base of the mountains near home appeared in his mind. The tall thin trees of the White Forest framed the village, separating them from the madness of the Ranvieg Mountain range. Kieron shivered as he pictured the ominous Black Mountains in the distance.

"You there. Halt!" ordered one of the guards that lined the hall.

Dangler held out his hand to halt the others.

The guard stepped in front of the group and inspected each one. "Wait here." The guard disappeared behind the door.

"Now, when we enter, let me do all the talking. You only speak when Valbrand speaks to you, understand?"

"Understood," Kieron replied. He cleared his throat.

Dangler turned to Kealy and Thyler, who were too frightened to speak. They simply stood with their mouths opened.

Dangler rolled his eyes, leaned forward, and tried to listen to what was happening on the other side of the door..

"Enter!" came the cry of the goblin, Valbrand's assistant. A potbellied beast, no higher than Dangler's knees, sauntered over to the three youths. "This way."

Kieron and Kealy glanced down at the goblin and followed it. "Dangler will remain behind." The goblin jerked his hand at the Dragon Master.

"Aren't you coming?" Kieron asked Dangler. "Why can't he come in with us?"

"Hush!" The goblin scowled.

Dangler shook his head. "Quiet. Valbrand wants to see you three alone." He sighed. "So be it."

The guard slammed the wooden door shut and the sound echoed through the room. The sound of water dripping down the cave walls broke the tension. The goblin stopped the youths, raised its hand, and hopped onto a large stone desk in the center of the bleak room. Behind the desk were bookcases filled with what looked like lodgers of some sort. Stacks and stacks of similar books lined the floor by the desk. Loose papers were scattered on the desk.

"What a slob," Kealy whispered.

"Shh," Kieron replied with a stern look.

The goblin lifted its chin and placed some reading spectacles onto its nose. He spoke. "Stand at attention!"

Kealy, Kieron, and Thyler obeyed.

A high-pitched grumbling voice was heard coming from an adjacent hall. "And make sure wine is served. Understand?" Valbrand shouted an order to his servant. "Don't disappoint me. We're expecting a grand crowd this time. Fruit juice won't suffice." He waved his hand and the servant exited the room.

Valbrand stopped and inspected the two elves and young boy

before him. He waved his hand again and the goblin hopped down off the desk. "Names." Valbrand leaned against the desk. His skeletal body showed underneath his tunic, which hung on him as though his frame were a hanger. One eye remained squinted shut while the other leered at Kieron. "Well?"

"Kieron Gaardoen of Glouslow, just outside the—"

"The White Forest, I know where that is." Valbrand sneered. "I'm not an idiot." He motioned for the goblin to bring him a shirt and coat off the rack in the corner. Valbrand took it and put on the white shirt first and buttoned the buttons at the wrists. Then he swung the thick coat around his body, sending some papers through the air from the breeze. He buttoned the coat at the waist and straightened it out. Next, he sat down behind a large wooden table, snapped his fingers, and snorted at the little goblin. The creature hobbled over to him and handed him a parchment paper.

"And you?" Valbrand turned to Kealy.

"I am Kealy Hauken of Rivermoor." She stood at attention.

"And you?" Valbrand looked Thyler up and down.

"I am Thyler of Heinland's Gate."

Valbrand's eyebrows rose. "The Dragon Master has informed me that your dragon riding skills are impressive." Valbrand read the parchment then tossed it aside. He stood and lumbered over to Kieron, leaning in toward him. "Who taught you?"

Kieron gulped. "My best friend."

Valbrand rolled his eyes. "Does this person have a name?"

"Kealy." Kieron nodded toward his friend.

"Ah, really?" Valbrand stepped in front of her. "So you taught the boy everything he knows?"

Kealy nodded yes, trying not to wince at the man's rancid breath.

But Valbrand seemed unconvinced. He jerked his head toward Kieron. "And what about your brother?" he asked Kieron.

His eyes widened. "Excuse me?"

"Sir!" the goblin shouted. "You will address the warden as sir."

"Excuse me, sir?"

"Théan Gaardoen? Isn't that your brother?" Valbrand crossed his arms.

All the blood drained from Kieron's head. His throat went as dry as the dirt floor. "I, uh…yes, that's my brother. But how did you know?"

Valbrand's mouth curled up into a snarl. "He participated in the Dragon Games a while back, did he not? Won his category and a place on the Queen's Dragon Riders. But unlike this boy's older brothers, before Thèan could head to the palace, he decided to test his skills inside the Great Arena. Didn't you know?" Valbrand handed the parchment to the goblin.

Kieron's mind raced. He knew his brother had been inside the prison but to rescue the dragons, or so he thought. Was he wrong about it? Did Théan fight in the arena? He opened his mouth but no words came out.

"When told your name, I wasn't surprised. I suspected Théan would want his younger brother to follow in his footsteps. Of course, once Prince Thætil discovered your brother's involvement in the games here, he was disqualified from being a Dragon Rider forever." Valbrand spun around. "You see, the queen despises what we do here inside this prison. She's fought us all the way, but she's no match for Lord Bedlam."

A chill ran through Kieron's body at the mention of the dark Lord's name.

"So, it appears you have a choice to make, young Kieron." Valbrand leaned on the stone desk. "If you fly in the Great Arena for me, you can earn much gold coin that could help your family. I've heard you're even better than your brother."

Kieron's eyes grew large.

"Yes, that's right. You're much better. Faster than he ever was. My spies told me."

Kealy looked over at Kieron who stood speechless.

"So, if you fly for me in the Great Arena, you could win and become a champion. But…"

"I will forfeit my chance to ride for the queen?" Kieron frowned.

Valbrand snickered.

The dragons, Kieron reminded himself. *It's not about the queen or games. The plan must go forward.* "If that's what it takes. I'll do it."

Kealy jerked her head toward Kieron.

"We both will, right?" Kieron turned to her. She slowly nodded, revealing her hesitancy.

But Kieron noticed she seemed to regain her composure.

"Of course." Kealy raised her chin. "If it means we can help our

"Valbrand, the Warden of Rünbrior Prison"

families and be champions, then so be it."

Kieron sighed with relief.

"Well, then," Valbrand continued, "We shall get you started right away." He waved the goblin assistant over to his side and murmured something in its ear. The tiny beast scooted away and exited the room. "Not you." Valbrand motioned toward Thyler. "You'll return to Dangler."

"But, we're a team." Kieron reached for Thyler's arm.

"Not him. Just you, two."

The guard entered and pulled Thyler out the door.

"He lacks the skill his brothers had...and the skills you have. You two will fight in the Great Arena tonight." Valbrand grinned a wry grin with his thin lips pressed against his sharp yellow teeth.

Kieron managed a smile, but his insides quaked. "We are ready, sir."

"I certainly hope so. Because of Dangler, I have wagered much gold on you." With that, Valbrand shouted an order to his guards who quickly entered the room. "Take them to the training area and fit them with gear. Move!"

The two guards grabbed Kieron and Kealy by their arms, practically lifting them off the floor, and moved them to the door, where an anxious Dangler waited.

"Get them to the training area to be fitted for gear." One guard pointed down another hallway.

Dangler bowed and stood with Kieron and Kealy as the guards returned to their posts outside Valbrand's quarters.

"Come now." Dangler motioned for the two elves to follow him. Kieron and Kealy obeyed and cautiously ventured down the hallway. The carved rock walls appeared smoother than the others and more torches lit the path. The sound of hammers against metal met them as they turned a corner. Bright fire light and heat hit their faces, causing them to raise their arms to protect their eyes.

"Come this way." Dangler headed toward a stack of armor. He grabbed a breastplate and held it to Kieron's chest to measure it. "This will have to do."

But Kieron hardly noticed. His eyes rested upon the blacksmith, hammering a sword, glowing red from the fire pit.

"Kieron," Dangler said. "Pay attention."

"By fighting in this arena, we are forfeiting our chance to be on the Dragon Riders." Kieron stared at Dangler. "Why didn't you tell us that?"

Dangler lowered the breastplate and whispered. "Because, Kieron, if you two succeed in freeing all the dragons and slaves inside this prison along with Prince Peter, I think the Queen will be willing to look past how you had to risk your lives by fighting in the Great Arena to do it."

Kieron nodded that he understood.

"Now hold steady!"

Kieron jerked his head around and nodded as he took the metal breastplate and slipped into it. The weight of the metal armor almost knocked him over.

"Aye, this is the trouble with asking boys to fight in the arena. There isn't any armor that fits." Dangler shook his head.

"That's alright," Kieron replied. He adjusted the breastplate as much as he could. "It'll work."

"Besides, we won't be wearing it for long, if all goes as planned." Kealy slipped into her breastplate.

A blacksmith stopped hammering and glanced their way.

"Shhh." Dangler winced and placed his hand over her mouth. "Not another word," he whispered and jerked his head toward the blacksmith.

"Sorry," Kealy mouthed the word underneath Dangler's hand. He slowly removed it.

"Come, let's get you a sword and helmet."

Kieron noticed the other blacksmiths had stopped hammering as well. They stared holes into his back as he left the area and entered yet another room with stacks of helmets, shields, and swords.

"Whew," Kieron said. "That was close."

Dangler grunted something and pointed to the stack of helmets. "Pick one out for yourself."

Kealy bent down to retrieve one that seemed smaller.

"Look," Kieron said. In his hands was a helmet with blood spatter on it. He tossed it down as though it were a poisonous snake.

"And this one." Kealy held up a helmet, burned black from dragon fire. Her eyes grew wide and Kieron understood her concern.

"We thought the dragon's fire glands were removed?" Kieron's voice quivered.

"Well, sometimes a dragon is missed during the process. What did you expect?" Dangler growled. "This isn't child's play. These are fierce dragons, trained to kill. Valbrand's dragon, Scythar still has her fire. And she doesn't hesitate to use it."

Kieron grabbed Dangler's arm. "We aren't fighting that dragon, are we?"

"Why are you concerned? You'll speak to the dragons, gain their trust, and we'll be on our way by then, deep within the caves, rescuing dragons and freeing the slaves. Come. Pick a sword, and let's begin our preparations for the arena."

"The Great Arena"

∽

Kieron gripped his sword as tightly as he could. The metal sword grew heavier and heavier as he and Kealy waited for the horn to blow and Dangler to wave them into the arena. Vâken squawked. Kieron was grateful to have his dragon with him.

The arena smelled of dirt, sweat, and dragon dung. Kieron wrinkled his nose.

The sword in his grip felt awkward. *I prefer bows and arrows.* He sighed. "Steady, Vâken," Kieron squeezed his thighs to let his dragon know he was there, atop his back, and would remain there throughout the battle. He gulped at the thought of what awaited them in the Great Arena.

"Listen to that crowd!" Kealy shouted above the fray.

Kieron nodded, causing his oversized helmet to tilt and momentarily block his view. Frustrated, he reached up and adjusted the metal headgear.

"Boy!" Dangler approached. "Listen to me."

Kieron leaned in.

"Pay attention. Look over there." Dangler motioned to some fighters standing at the entrance. "That is the opponent you need to be concerned with." He singled out one young man.

Kieron noticed the lanky young man, wearing the black armor of Rünbrior.His posture revealed his confidence. *He isn't afraid,* Kieron thought. *Why should I be?*

"What is his name?" Kealy asked.

"What difference does that make?" Dangler asked.

"A name means something." Kealy turned to him.

"Damon. Damon of Doerfshire." Dangler replied. "He is one of the best fighters. He has battled Ethan of Riverdale many time."

"Doerfshire. Nice rolling hills there. Excellent dragon riders come from that region." Kealy nodded toward Kieron.

"He battles Prince Peter?" Kieron whispered to Dangler. "If he is the prince."

"Aye."

"Where is his dragon?" Kieron searched the area.

"He fights on foot along with those men." Dangler pointed to several armored men standing in the entrance to the arena. "And he's very good. And clever, so watch him."

Dangler pointed in another direction. "You will face men on dragons. They enter from the other side of the arena. Fly fast and be quick in action, but be aware of the men on the ground. They will try to attack you, too. Stay alive at all costs and talk to the dragons!

Win here and you'll move to the next battle, where the bigger dragons fight. We need them."

"Understood," Kieron replied.

"Now, it is time. Fly out and face your opponents as they come from the other side. Use your dragonspeak. Gain their trust. You'll see!" Dangler swatted the backside of Vâken, stirring the dragon. It roared and flapped its wings to take flight. "Stay alive!"

Kealy heeled her dragon's ribs and the beast flapped its wings to follow Vâken. "Here we go!"

The roar of the crowd electrified Kieron. It was if the thousand voices lifted him and Vâken higher into the air. The passion of the crowd fueled his desire to win the battle inside the Great Arena. It was everything he thought it would be. The enormous cave carved from within the mountain reached as high as it was wide. The walls had caves carved out where some spectators sat, eating fruit and drinking ale and wine. One large cave housed Valbrand and his ilk, raising steins and mugs overflowing with ale.

Kieron's eyes met Valbrand's, and the two nodded.

"To battle!" Kieron's opponent shouted as he approached atop a lythe Draco, much larger than Vâken, who roared back.

"Spew your fire and then spin down!" Kieron ordered and Vâken obeyed, releasing a stream of fire. The opponent jerked his dragon out of the way. Then, Vâken and Kieron fell as one, spinning toward the arena floor where the fighters stood, facing each other. When the horn blew, Vâken flapped his wings, sending him and Kieron up and over the crowd. They roared their approval of the move.

"This way!" Kealy flew past, waving for Kieron to follow her. She raised her sword.

Kieron was about to respond, when his helmet tilted toward the front again, blocking his view. "No!" he shouted, reaching up, and removing the annoying headgear. He tossed it to the ground.

"What are you doing?" Kealy scowled at him.

"I know what I'm doing. Let's go!" Kieron nudged Vâken and leaned in close to its neck, gripping his sword even tighter.

Kealy followed after him and the two attacked their opponents, swiping at them with their swords. The other dragons spun out and soared above them.

"Uh oh." Kieron recognized the move. "Split up!"

Kealy obeyed and turned her dragon to the left as Kieron turned Vâken to the right. They swooped out of the way of the oncoming dragons just in time to miss the swords of the riders.

"Whew!" Kieron pulled on the reins and Vâken flew back around to face off with the opponents. With sword in hand, Kieron raised his arm back as they approached. He started to swipe at the dragon rider and the crowd roared its approval.

"Speak to the dragon!" Kealy shouted as she passed by.

"Oh yeah." Kieron turned Vâken around and the two swooped toward the opposing rider again, to the cheers of the crowd.

This is easier than I thought. Maybe I should make this last a little longer. He bent low to Vâken's head. "Let's give them a show!" The dragon snorted and squawked.

"I know I need to speak to the dragons, but we also need to impress Valbrand."

Vâken quickly flew toward the crowd again. He dove over one group of spectators waving their hands and flags in the air. *This must be what my brother feels like when his fans cheer him.* Kieron smiled at the crowd.

Kealy and her dragon hovered high near the ceiling of the giant arena, watching the scene. The light from the torches reflected in her dragon's scales. Kealy, too, dove toward the crowd atop her dragon and swooped over them, causing the crowd to duck. They hopped up and cheered for Kealy.

"Not a bad show, huh?" Kieron shouted toward her.

"What are you doing? Did you speak to the dragons? Did they not understand?" She shouted.

"No! They don't seem to understand me." Kieron lied. Vâken turned and glared at him. Kieron shrugged. But then he saw the opponents with their angry glares. "Uh oh."

He and Kealy prepared their dragons to face off with the opponents, charging at them at high speed.

"Steady!" he urged. "On the count of three, follow me!"

The dragon riders flew faster and faster, heading toward Kieron and Kealy.

"Three…two…now!" Kieron pulled the reins back, heeled Vâken's ribs, and shot straight up. Kealy's dragon followed suit. As a result, the two dragon riders approaching them shot straight forward, missing Kieron and Kealy.

The crowd, again, roared its approval.

The horn blasted, ending the battle, and all the dragon riders returned to where they had started. Dangler rushed over to Kieron and Vâken, taking the little dragon's bridle into his hand. "Well done."

Kieron hopped off and patted Vâken's head. "That was easier than I thought it would be!"

Kealy hopped off her dragon and ran over to Kieron. "That was disappointing."

"What happened?" Dangler asked.

"Kieron said the dragons didn't understand him." Kealy frowned.

"When do we get to do it again?" Kieron shouted above the applause of the crowd as the men on the arena floor battled one another. "We put on quite the show!"

"Oooh!" the crowd shouted.

Kieron turned to see that one fighter had impaled another with a spear, ending the man's life.

"It isn't all a show," Dangler reminded Kieron. "Come, let's head to the cave."

As he watched the crowds cheer the death of a man, Kieron swallowed hard. *That could have been me.* Kieron turned to Kealy and noticed she had the same look of fear on her face.

"Follow me!" A guard shouted, startling Kieron. It was one of Valbrand's guards.

Kieron searched for Dangler to tell him the truth but he was already down the hall, walking Vâken back to the cave for rest.

"Where are you taking us?" Kealy asked.

"Just follow me," the guard replied. "The warden wants to see you." He spun around and walked off in a different direction.

"What should we do?" Kieron asked Kealy.

"I think we should do as he says." Kealy made her way down

the hallway until they reached some steps.

"This way." The guard motioned for them to head up the stone steps.

Kieron and Kealy entered the darkened stairway, still able to hear the crowd cheering on the next battle. They walked until the stairway opened up to one of the caves, carved out of the arena walls. Reclining on a balcony while overlooking the battle, sat Valbrand. He gulped down ale from a elaborately carved stein and plopped it down onto a tray. He was about to order more ale be brought to him when he spied Kieron and Kealy in the entryway.

"Welcome!" He waved them over to the balcony. His guests also leaned over the edge to watch the fighters battle below them. "Here they are, my two champions."

Valbrand's guests applauded Kieron and Kealy as they made their way across the cave room, adorned with tapestries on the walls and woven carpets on the floor. Trays of fruits and breads rested on wooden tables, and a harpist strummed a tune on her harp. Kieron perked up as the people praised his riding skill.

Kealy moved out of the way as one woman tried to touch her braided hair.

"I've never seen such lovely white hair before," said the woman.

"Yes, well, it's mine so please don't touch it." Kealy offered her a weak smile.

"Come sit here." Valbrand ordered his goblin to place a chair next to him, but the little creature struggled to move the wooden chair. Kieron rushed over to assist.

He and Kealy slowly sat down across from their host, the warden of Rünbrior prison. Kieron tried to swallow the lump in his throat, but the fear inside him wouldn't allow it.

"You both performed as I knew you would. The crowd loved the show!" Valbrand shouted. His guests applauded once again.

"Thank you." Kieron grinned widely.

"Here's the gold I will have my servants send to your families." The goblin held up two bags and opened them so Valbrand could remove a few gold coins. "I am certain your families will appreciate the gold."

Kealy's eyes grew large as the gold sparkled in the firelight.

"And if you fly for me again tomorrow, even more gold will be sent to them."

Kieron's mouth dropped open. *Gold.*

"Just imagine what your families could do with all this gold!" Valbrand turned to his guests. "Just imagine!"

They, once again, applauded on cue.

Kealy leaned in to whisper in Kieron's ear. "But the plan…"

Kieron couldn't take his eyes off the gold. *My father would have to approve of me once he sees all this gold.*

Valbrand removed more coins and shuffled them with his bony hands. His eyes narrowed to mere slits as he stared at Kieron, mesmerized by the gold.

"What say you?" Valbrand asked.

"Yes!" Kieron shouted.

Kealy turned to him. *"What?"*

"Wonderful! Tomorrow you'll perform in the arena again." Valbrand reached over and slapped Kieron on the back. Then he waved for his guard to take Kieron away, leaving Kealy alone.

"And what about you, my dear?" Kieron heard Valbrand ask Kealy. He turned to see her looking at Valbrand and then at him with a look of desperation.

Just agree to it, he mouthed to his friend.

"Alright," she said in a small voice.

"Excellent!" Valbrand touched her cheek. Kealy winced and moved out of his way. "Take her and the boy to my special quarters."

"Special quarters?" Kieron asked.

Valbrand nodded his head as he gulped down more ale. Spit trickled down his chin. He reached up and wiped it with his tunic sleeve. "Yes! Special sleeping quarters for all my prize dragon riders. Away with you both."

CHAPTER 8

Kealy leaned in close to Kieron. "Are you out of your mind?" she whispered they followed the guard down the steps. "Shhh," he ordered her. "He'll hear you!"

"I don't care. We made a promise to help Dangler." Kealy stomped down the steps.

Kieron remained silent the rest of the way, thinking of his father working the farm. "This gold will help my family," he finally said to Kealy as they approached a large wooden doorway that reached more than ten feet above them. "That's all that matters now."

She crossed her arms and frowned at him.

The guard pushed on both doors, swinging them open. The space before them was grand indeed. "This is where you'll remain until morning, when you fight in the arena again."

He shoved Kealy and Kieron inside and slammed the doors shut behind them. The jolt of the doors slamming made Kealy wince. She stood directly in front of Kieron.

"Are you mad? You must be mad. How can you possibly want to stay here and fly for that creepy old warden?" She tossed her hands into the air. "You are insane. You have to be!"

But Kieron glanced around the space with its ornate sconces on the wall, bear skin rugs on the floor, and overstuffed pillows on the large beds. "Look at those beds!" he shouted as he ran over to one. He plopped down and practically disappeared as the soft feather mattress enveloped him. "Ahhhhh…" He reclined back and closed his eyes.

Kealy plopped down onto a chair and continued to sulk. "Just wait until Dangler hears about this."

Kieron sat up and struggled to get out the bed. "What are you so angry about?"

"We made a promise to Dangler!" Kealy huffed.

"Look, I tried to speak to the dragons. It didn't work. Dangler will understand when he sees all that gold being sent to our families." Kieron made his way over to a tray full of fruit. He picked up an apple and bit into it, savoring the sweet juiciness of it.

"Have an apple." He tossed one over to Kealy, who caught it and promptly set it down. "Ah, come on." Kieron sat by her.

"How can you just forget about the plan like that? And for what? A piece of fruit? A soft bed?" Kealy stood and walked away from him.

"Gold! For all that gold!"

The door opened and one of Valbrand's guards appeared.

"The warden wants to see you," he said to Kieron. "Alone."

"Alone?" Kealy asked.

"Alone." The guard glared at her.

Kieron stepped over to the guard and followed him out the door.

Once inside Valbrand's quarters, Kieron nervously stood near the door.

"Come here, my boy." Valbrand waved over to him as soon as he entered the space. He removed his coat and tossed it onto a chair. "Sit. Enjoy some refreshments. I tell you, I have not seen a young elf fly as well as you do."

"Thank you." Kieron glanced around the large room with it's tapestries on the walls, gold chandeliers, and ornante gilt tables with matching chairs.

"What do you think of your new quarters, eh?" Valbrand brought over a tray filled with fruit and bread. "Not too shabby, huh?"

"The room is very nice, thank you." Kieron selected some cinnamon bread and munched on it.

"Tasty?" Valbrand sat across from him.

"Very."

"I have my own baker and chef prepare delicious meals for me." He winked. "Do you look forward to flying more often in the arena?"

Kieron nodded and then frowned.

"What is it?"

But Kieron didn't reply.

"Tell me. I have the power to make all your wishes come true." Valbrand downed some wine.

"I wish for nothing, but…" Kieron hesitated.

"But what?" Valbrand smiled, revealing his tiny yellow teeth.

"For the dragons in here to be treated much better than they are."

Valbrand slammed down his pewter cup. "Bah!" Some of his spittle flew through the air. "My dragons are well cared for."

"Not the dragons I have seen. They are malnourished and weak. They are in cages and are sad." Kieron set down his slice of bread.

Valbrand shook his head. "No, no. Not my dragons. Those are Dangler's dragons. He mistreats the ones who refuse to be trained. He beats and cages the dragons that lose in the arena."

Kieron thought about it. "But…that's not true, is it?"

"The dragons under *my* care are healthy and strong. It is Dangler who abuses the dragons." Valbrand stood.

"I..I can't believe that." Kieron thought more about what he had seen and what Dangler had told him. *Could he have been lying to me?*

Valbrand waved Kieron over to a side door. "Don't believe me? Come and see for yourself."

Kieron rose and followed after Valbrand through a long hallway that led to a large cave with many stables. In each stable was a dragon. They were big, strong, and healthy, with black scales. Thick horns protruded from their heads and all the way down their backs.

"These are my prize dragons." Valbrand proudly waved his hand in the air. "They serve me well so I take good care of them."

Kieron made his way by each stall, studying the dragons carefully. Their sturdy muscular legs were impressive as were their enormous wings. He stood before one and leaned in close to it. "Ush myiel," he whispered to it. But it did not react to his dragonspeak.

He noticed the eyes of the dragon seemed odd, unlike anything he had ever seen. Its pupils were mere slits. But Valbrand was right and his dragons were well cared for. Kieron suspected Dangler was lying to him.

Back in Valbrand's room, Kieron sat back down at the table. "Dangler told me all the dragons within this prison are tortured."

Valbrand laughs. "Dangler is mad."

"He also said that there's a rumor about the prince of Illiath. He is inside this prison." Kieron selected another slice of cinnamon bread.

Valbrand laughed again. "A silly rumor, that's all."

"But Dangler said the boy Ethan of Riverdale is quite the fighter inside the arena and just might be the prince in disguise."

Valbrand leaned in close to Kieron. "Do you see how crazy Dangler is? Ethan is just a farm boy who excels in the Great Arena and you Kieron can, too." He winked again.

When Kieron finished his bread and juice, he returned to his room where Kealy sat, fuming.

"You should see how big Valbrand's room is. And his dragons! They are well cared for." Kieron shouted when he entered the room.

Kealy stared daggers into him. "Valbrand is evil. All he cares about is getting rich."

"That's not true. His dragons are healthy and strong, not like Dangler's dragons." Kieron chortled.

The door swung open and slammed against the wall, revealing Dangler, seething with anger.

Kealy ran over to him. "This was all Kieron's idea. I just went along with it because—"

"Hush!" Dangler shouted. He raised his cane and jabbed it at Kieron.

"Look, I tried to speak to those dragons, but they didn't understand me, so I flew to entertain the crowd. You know, to impress Valbrand, so we can fly again tomorrow. It worked!" Kieron smiled.

But Dangler and Kealy frowned.

"I'll try and speak to the dragons again, I promise." Kieron grabbed an apple and bit into it.

"Your promises are worth less and less each hour." Dangler glared at him.

"It will work, I promise—er, I mean, I just need more time. One more chance to try the dragonspeak."

"You're lying."

"You lie, too!"

"What are you talking about?" Dangler shouted.

"Valbrand takes care of his dragons. They are healthy and

strong. Your dragons are sick. You're the one mistreating dragons."

"Valbrand's dragons are under a spell." Dangler jabbed his finger at him.

"He says he takes care of them. I have seen them and it's true." Kieron tossed the apple aside.

"Don't be a fool! All Valbrand cares about is himself." Dangler hobbled toward the door.

"I don't believe you." Kieron crossed his arms.

Dangler squinted at Kieron. "You. Come with me!"

Kieron slowly followed after him. "Where are we going?" "Just come with me," Dangler grumbled. "I've something to show you."

"I'll stay here." She watched the two head out the door and into the darkened hallway.

"Where are we going, Dangler?" Kieron asked.

But Dangler remained silent as he walked in front of Kieron, leading him further down the hallway. He paused at a doorway that had a stairway heading down.

"What's this?" Kieron asked. "Are you ever going to answer me?"

Dangler kept walking down the steps, once in a while he'd wipe his nose, but he remained eerily silent until the stairway opened to a larger space filled with enormous cages that held dragons of all shapes and sizes. Most squawked from fear and desperation, but many rushed the cage walls to snap at Kieron and Dangler as they walked by.

Kieron fell back, afraid for his life, when he saw the dragons claw at him. The fierce anger in their eyes revealed their hatred toward man and elf.

"What is this place?" Kieron asked.

"The dungeon," he replied. "For dragons. Valbrand's dragons."

Kieron gulped as he watched one dragon bang its head against the metal bars of the cage over and over again. Its blood dripped from a gash in its head. Another dragon sat coiled up, shivering in the corner of one cage, only staring straight ahead at nothing. Her scales littered the cage floor. Kieron could tell she had given up and was near death. He glanced away.

"Don't turn away, boy!" Dangler reached up and grabbed Kieron's face. He forced him to look at the poor dragon. "Look at the beast!"

But Kieron backed away.

"What's the matter?" Dangler shouted at him. "I thought you spoke to dragons? What are they saying to you now, boy?"

Tears formed in Kieron's eyes. He had never seen such anger in Dangler's face.

"Are they worth all that gold coin? Well, are they?" Dangler pointed to the dragons roaring inside the cages, desperately trying to spew their fire from glands that were brutally removed. "Look at them! This is what happens to Valbrand's dragons once he is finished with them."

Kieron raised his eyes toward all the abused creatures within the cages. There were over thirty of them. He covered his mouth to keep from vomiting from the smell and sight.

Dangler stood before Kieron. "We had a plan, boy. You vowed to be part of that plan to help free these creatures and the slaves within these prison walls."

"The Dungeon"

Kieron stared into the eyes of one dragon. It could barely lift its head off the ground. Its back was covered in scars that had healed, one over another.

"I cannot do it alone. I need your help. Or are you sold out for Valbrand now?" Dangler turned away and headed for the steps.

"No!" Kieron followed after him. "I'm sorry! I let it get to my head. Don't leave me in here!"

Dangler turned to him. "You don't owe me an apology, boy. You owe them."

Kieron turned to the dragons. "Ish niender then il undrath!" he shouted at them, then fell to his knees.

Dangler squinted his eyes and watched him.

The larger dragons stopped roaring. Their heads tilted left and then right.

"Non nothriél," Kieron said in a voice barely above a whisper. "Please forgive me. Is allthrien ul vas nathrâ. Nathras vien. Il ish niél."

"What are you telling them?" Dangler asked.

Kieron stood and slowly approached the cage of the one dragon that appeared near death. He placed his hand on the cage bars. "Il ish niél." He sniffled as the dragon turned her head to him. "I'm telling them all how sorry I am and I'm begging them to believe me when I say I will free them."

The weakened dragon, a Wyvern with tattered wings, hobbled over to him and sniffed his hand, gripping the metal bars.

"Il isn niél. Uth vas ilien. Mythrien uth vas." Kieron's tears fell to the ground. "I am asking her to hold on a little while longer and I will set her free. She is near death."

Dangler hung his head low.

Kieron approached the larger dragons. "I will need your help!" he begged them. "Vestude il ilien dobré mythiel ul ién!"

They raised their heads high and roared, tossing Kieron's hair back from the force of their roars.

Dangler stepped back. "Well, what was their reply?"

Kieron laughed and stroked the snout of one of the beasts. "They said they will help us only if they are allowed to kill and eat Valbrand."

Dangler chortled. "Come now, let's get Kealy, and the two of you can plan how to—"

"Not so fast," came a voice from the stairway.

Dangler and Kieron turned to see who spoke.

Kieron's eyes widened when he saw it was his brother, Théan.

"What are you doing here?" Kieron asked.

"I'm here to take you home, you little brat." Théan said with a sneer.

"What?" Kieron approached his brother.

"Come on!" Théan gripped Kieron's arm and dragged him into the stairway. "I'm taking you home."

"No!" Kieron struggled to get free. "Not now." The dragons in the cages roared their disapproval of the scene.

"Now, you see here!" Dangler rushed over to Kieron and grabbed his other arm. He and Théan used Kieron as a rope in a strange tug-o-war. "The boy stays here!"

"He's coming home with me. Our father is angry enough as it is." Théan won the war and shoved Kieron into the darkened hall, where he spied Théan's friends, ready to take him home against his will.

"No! The dragons! We've got to free the dragons!" Kieron shouted. "I promised them!"

He turned to see the weak dragon turn away in despair and return to her corner, shivering again.

"No! They'll die in here. We have to free them." Kieron struggled to get free, but it was no use. Théan and his friends were too strong. "I made them a promise."

"Well, then you lied to them," Théan replied.

"You're making a big mistake," Dangler shouted after them. "The plan is already set in motion."

"You leave us alone, you old dwarf. Our father wants Kieron back home. Our home is more important than these dragons," Théan said with a sneer.

"With the Darkness over the land, there will be no more homes for any of you!" Dangler directed them to the cages. "These beasts will be the only way we can fight the Darkness." He moved toward Théan. "I remember you. You won the Dragon Games but you came in here to fly for Valbrand instead of the Queen. But Valbrand let you escape. Why?"

"Yes, and now I have returned to save my foolish little brother from Valbrand." Théan smirked at Kieron.

"How do you know you won't be caught this time?" Dangler moved closer to him.

"I know all the secret passages inside this prison." Théan chortled. "I flew for Valbrand once and lost my place on the Queen's Dragon Riders, that is true."

Dangler smirked in triumph.

"But I did it to help the prisoners and dragons escape."

"What?" Kieron stared at his brother. "You did?"

"Yeah, and when I saw that it was an act of futility, I got out of here," Théan said. "I returned home to tell the town leaders about the true dragon games within these walls. And when the time is right, my fellow elves will return to take it all away from Valbrand," Théan replied.

"The time is right now!" Dangler stomped his foot. "Valbrand isn't the one to worry about. It is Lord Bedlam who runs everything within this mountain prison."

"You're insane if you think you alone can stop the evil already set in motion." Théan pushed Kieron up the steps.

"No!" Kieron struggled, but to no avail. The last thing he heard coming from that dungeon were the roars of the captive dragons.

Théan shoved Kieron down another hallway that led to a cave, facing the mountain precipice. Five dragons waited near the cave opening, and each elf climbed atop one and took off. Théan placed Kieron onto his saddle and sat behind him, grasping his waist tightly to keep him from leaping off right as the dragon dove off the cliff, heading toward Glouslow.

Home again.

Théan's dragon landed, and Kieron quickly hopped off. His boots sank into the deep mud.

"You have no idea what you've just done," Kieron cried.

"Sure I do. I saved you, little brother, from becoming a slave for Valbrand." Théan guided his dragon along by the reins, leading it to the cave where other dragons rested. The clopping sound of Théan's boots rising in and out of the mud echoed over the crows cawing above.

Crows. Kieron watched them circle above. *Bedlam's spies. He's watching us.*

"Now go inside the house. Father's waiting for you." Théan

walked on.

"The gold could have helped Mother and Father!" Kieron shouted to the back of his brother. "You idiot."

Théan turned around. "Idiot? Me? You're the idiot if you think you ever would have seen any of that gold."

Kieron tilted his head.

"Yes, that's right. Valbrand promised you gold, but he never would have sent it to Mother and Father. You're the foolish one."

Kieron's eyes filled with tears, but he blinked them away. "That cannot be. I saw the gold with my own eyes. Kealy did, too!"

Kealy. Her face suddenly came to Kieron's mind. He covered his weary eyes. "Oh no. Kealy remains inside that prison."

Théan rolled his eyes. "You are looking at someone who almost fell for the lies of Valbrand. But I got away." He pointed to his own chest. "Now look at what you've done. Your foolishness has hurt Kealy, your friend. What were you thinking, going after those bandits in the forest? You should've come told me about it."

"You would have laughed at me." Kieron wiped his nose. "You always laugh at me."

"Maybe so. But at least Kealy would still be here."

"But the dragons…I promised to save them." Kieron lowered his head.

"Yes, well, they're stuck in there, and you're out here."Théan sighed. "Well, come on now. We've got to go in and tell Father all that has happened."

As they walked toward the little house with the candlelight in the window, Kieron felt that familiar burning in his gut. He knew his father hated him and blamed him for Aislinn's death, but now…he knew his father would probably send him away to live with his aunt and uncle in Illiath, after all the trouble he'd caused the family. One thing was for certain, there'd be no more dragon riding ever again . Kieron sighed. He didn't care. He'd simply pack up his things and take his dragons with him to live in the woods somewhere. He was a dragon rider and nothing would ever change that.

Nothing.

They stood together in front of the house. Théan patted Kieron's shoulder. "Go on, take my dragon to its stall. I'll do my best to try and explain things. Maybe Father won't be too angry if I explain *why* you did what you did," Théan said. "Give me a few minutes to smooth things over."

"Alright." With his head hung low, Kieron took the panting dragon to the cave. He tossed some fresh hay onto the ground, made sure all the dragons inside had water, and removed the lid to the barrel of fish.

Théan's dragon had already turned in a circle and plopped down onto the fresh hay to sleep. It tucked its legs underneath its body and covered itself with its wings. The weak and sick dragon in the cage appeared in his mind. "You're the lucky one," he said to the dragon. "The other dragons remain imprisoned within that mountain."

Kieron wiped his eyes. *What was I thinking? Théan's right. I am foolish to think that I could spare any dragon an awful life and death in the dragon games. And now poor Kealy is still there. How can I ever get back inside to free her?*

As he exited the cave and faced the house, he wondered if Théan had had enough time to calm his father down. If not, he was more than prepared to fly away on a dragon tonight. He knew just where he'd fly to. His favorite fishing hole outside of Vulgaard between Pike's mountain and the land of Dwarves. He'd found the fishing hole two summers ago and went there when his father ordered him to go hunting and fishing. It was his favorite place to fish, relax, and dream of being a dragon rider for the queen.

The door.

That's all that separated him from his father. *Would he ever forgive me for Aislinn's death?* Kieron wondered. *And now would he forgive me for this mess that I've created?* He breathed in some courage, reached for the door handle, and pried it open.

"Kieron!" screamed his mother right before a Rider of Rünbrior covered her mouth with his large hand.

She sat, tied with rope, to a chair. Next to her was his father, also bound with rope to a chair. Théan lay on the ground, unconscious. Four Riders stood in the kitchen, staring at Kieron. He stepped back, but another Rider was behind him. He slammed the door shut, startling Kieron almost out of his skin. He clutched his chest and tried to breathe. They each wore the dark leather breastplates of Rünbrior and masks that covered the top half of their faces, but their evil eyes could be seen through slits in their masks. Black deep-set eyes that glared into Kieron's soul.

"What...what do you want?" Kieron said.

"I think you know what we want," the leader said. He slowly removed his gloves and stuffed them into his belt.

"I don't know what you mean," Kieron lied. He knew exactly why they were there.

"You made a promise to Valbrand." The leader grinned.

"And I meant to keep it. Honestly. My brother here forced me to go with him." Kieron tried to swallow but his throat became so dry, it gagged him.

"Valbrand gave us orders to bring you to back to the prison," the leader said.

"Mmmm!" Kieron's mother shook her head no and tried to scream. Tears streamed down her face. His father wrestled against the ropes that wrapped around his arms and chest. He shook his head at Kieron.

"Or what?" Kieron knew the answer.

One Rider removed a long blade from its sheath and held it to Kieron's father's throat.

"We'll kill your family, burn down this house, and the farm," the leader said.

Kieron, without hesitating, held out his hands. The Rider behind him shackled them. He winced from the pain of the metal cuffs around both wrists.

"Nnnnnn!" his father tried to scream, but the cloth in his mouth prevented him. It was for the best. If they did scream, Kieron knew the Riders would be merciless.

"It'll be alright, Father," Kieron said. "I have to keep my promise." But inside his mind, Kieron knew he'd have to find Dangler and Kealy again and put the plan into motion. Oh, he'd pretend to be there to fight in the arena for Valbrand's gold, but it was Valbrand's turn to be the foolish one.

The leader laughed. "Get him out of here."

They turned him around by the shoulders and shoved him out the door. The last image of home Kieron saw was his mother's weeping face.

Once out in the night, he smelled smoke. To his left rose bright yellow flames high into the sky. "No!" Kieron tried to wrestle free from the Riders, but one picked him up. He kicked and screamed when he saw the cave engulfed in flames. The roars of the dragons inside their stalls echoed throughout the land. All Kieron could think of was dragons trapped and burning inside their stalls.

"No! Let them go! They've done nothing to you!" he screamed.

"Shut up," the leader said. He lifted his hand and struck Kieron across the face.

Everything went dark.

"Riders of Rünbrior"

CHAPTER 9

Muffled sounds and the cold stone ground woke Kieron. He slowly pried open his heavy eyelids and blinked until everything came into focus.

"He's awake," said a man's voice. "Get him up!"

A man grabbed him from under his arms and stood Kieron up. He did his best to stand on weakened legs as he glanced around the space. When he realized where he was, his knees went weak.

"Straighten up!" the man shouted. Kieron obeyed.

"Get these scum moving!" The man ordered the guards.

Before he knew it, the entire line of prisoners began to move. Kieron noticed how most of the prisoners were his age. *Where are they taking us?*

The line of prisoners moved through a well-lit tunnel, lined with shields, quivers of arrows, swords, and armor strewn about, making Kieron nervous. It smelled of sweat and dank air.

Ahead, the tunnel ended. Several rather large men, wearing armor, stood at the opening, holding swords and shields.

"Stand still," a guard ordered them. He then went down the line and unlocked the metal cuffs on their wrists. "Stack all the swords and shields over there. And gather up the quivers. Go!"

The line of boys raced around, doing what was asked of them. But Kieron, still dizzy from being hit across the head, didn't move right away. He tried to get his bearings first.

"You there, move it!" the guard shouted into his ear.

Kieron turned and began picking up stray arrows, placing them inside quivers. But a ferocious roar coming from outside the tunnel stopped him as though frozen.

What was that? He looked left and right but no one seemed

concerned. Another roar came, and the ground beneath his feet shook.

The sound of cheers and shouts could be heard, rising from outside the tunnel. The activity inside the tunnel became chaotic as men raced around as though preparing for something.

"Line up!" one guard shouted at the men. The immediately obeyed.

"Dragons," the boy next to him said.

"Why isn't anyone concerned that a rather large dragon is on the loose out there?" Kieron asked.

The boy shook his head. "Do you know where you are?" He jerked his thumb over his shoulder. "That's the Great Arena out there."

Kieron desperately tried to focus his eyes, but his head still ached, making his vision a bit blurry. He snuck over to the tunnel opening. The guards and men were too distracted to notice him. That's when he saw the spectacle.

Rows and rows of people from all over Vulgaard and beyond sat in the stands made of stone. They stood on their feet, clapping and cheering as the fighters trotted out onto the arena floor. That's when he spotted Dangler approaching.

"Yes," Kieron mumbled.

"You there! Get back over here before I give you the lash!" one guard shouted. He grabbed Kieron by the collar and pulled him over to the middle of the space.

"Hold on, there," a gruff voice said. Out came Dangler from behind the man. "I'll take this one."

The guard turned and inspected the Dragon Master before him. "This scrawny thing?"

"That's the elf boy who had escaped," another guard said.

Kieron wriggled free from the man's grip.

"He's all mine. He's going to pay for what he did!" Dangler shouted and took Kieron by the arm.

"But…you…" Kieron gulped.

"Shh," Dangler whispered. "Come with me."

"Go ahead. He's all yours. Feed him to your dragons!" The man laughed. "That's what I'd do."

"Not much a meal for them, though," another man said.

"Come on, boy," Dangler ordered as he shoved Kieron aside.

"This way."

Kieron hastily walked in the direction Dangler had pointed him. Soon, they faced a wooden door. "Where's Kealy? Is she alright?"

Dangler removed keys from his belt and unlocked it. "Hurry. Get inside." Dangler glanced down the hall as though concerned they were followed.

Inside the room, lit by torches in sconces on the walls, stood Kealy with her arms crossed. Kieron ran to her, but she backed away from him.

"Kealy, I am so sorry," he begged, but it was no use. She wouldn't even look him in the eye.

"Sit," Dangler commanded. Kieron pulled up the wooden stool and sat down.

Kieron sat with his head hung down. "I'm so sorry for everything."

Kealy finally looked his way.

"I allowed my selfishness to get in the way of the plan, and ruined everything," he whispered.

"Oh that's not true." Kealy rushed toward him, hugging his shoulders. "You were only thinking of your family."

Kieron wiped his nose with his sleeve. "No, I was thinking of myself." He stood and turned to Dangler. "Is the plan still on?"

"Well, since those other dragons out there didn't understand you when you spoke to them in dragonspeak, I'm not sure our plan can continue. We might have to think of another way to get those dragons to trust us enough to help." Dangler slammed one fist into his other hand. Kieron could see the frustration on the Dragon Master's face.

"I, um…" Kieron began. "Well, I don't know if they understand me or not."

"What?" Kealy turned toward him.

"The girl said you tried your dragonspeak but the dragons didn't understand you." Dangler squinted his eyes.

Kieron swung his arms, playfully. "I may have lied about that." He winced.

"You what?" Kealy rushed toward him with clenched fists. "You lied to me?"

Kieron bit his upper lip and nodded. He did all he could to avoid her large eyes. "Yes."

She took hold of his tunic and shoved him back. "How could you?"

Dangler quickly stepped between them.

"I'm in this horrid place because of you and you lied to me?" Kealy spun around and kick the leg of a chair, sending it flying across the room.

Kieron rubbed his arms as he watched his angry friend fume. "I know and I'm sorry."

"Why?" Kealy asked without turning around to face him. "Why did you lie about the dragons?"

"I wanted to keep flying." Kieron stared at the dirt floor. "I enjoyed the crowd cheering me and the excitement of it all. I didn't want it to end."

Kealy sighed. "Oh, Kieron."

"For once, the crowd was cheering me and not..." He hesitated. "Not my brother or Aislinn."

Kealy rubbed her forehead. "Kieron," she began, "You make it so difficult to stay angry with you."

Dangler made his way over to Kieron. "So, then you don't know if the dragons can understand you or not?"

Kieron shook his head.

"Then the plan is back on!" Dangler slapped his thighs.

"Really?" Kealy asked.

"Yes. The boy can try his dragonspeak on those other dragons and get them on our side." Dangler pointed toward the door. "Hear that commotion?"

Kieron nodded.

"That's Valbrand's dragon, Scathar, in the arena battling the Prince." Dangler narrowed his eyes. "He's out there fighting against a fire-breathing dragon with nothing to protect him but the Dragon's scale as a shield."

Kieron's eyebrows rose.

"That's right. Ethan of Riverdale *is* Prince Peter. Tired of hiding in this prison, he made his name known for all to hear. Now, he's out there fighting for his life. He's not concerned with gold coin or glory. No, he's out there fighting to save us all!" Dangler turned to face Kieron. "Now, are you ready this time to help me free the dragons?"

"Yes!" Kieron raced to the door.

"We both are." Kealy joined him.

"Good! To the dungeons first." Dangler threw open the door and glanced left, then right. "No guards. They're all busy watching the arena. Now's our chance. Let's go."

∽

As they headed out the door, Kieron heard the crowd cheer. He left Dangler's side to peek at the action in the arena.

When he did, he saw Prince Peter and the other fighters facing the largest dragon Kieron had ever seen.

Scathar, a giant Wyvern dragon, spread its wings wide, intimidating the opponents lined before it.

"What is that?" Kieron mouthed.

"That is Scathat. Valbrand's prize dragon," Dangler replied as he stood next to Kieron.

Prince Peter and his companion successfully dodged the beast. In his arms, the prince held the scale of the Dragon of the Forest.

"Look!" Kealy shouted. "He holds a shield unlike any I have ever seen before."

"It is the scale of the Dragon of the Forest." Kieron couldn't take his eyes off of it.

Kealy turned to Kieron. "A what?"

"Remain steady," Prince Peter shouted to his friend in the arena. Kieron and Kealy watched as Prince Peter raised his hand up to calm the other fighters, but never took his eyes off Scathar. The dragon clawed at the ground. The crowd roared its approval. Then it leaned its head back and roared, causing the walls to tremble. Kieron leaned on a large bolder to steady himself.

Scathar was ready to begin the battle. Spikes adorned the sides of her narrow face and all the way down her back. Thick browbones that began from her nostrils all the way across her head and encased her deepset eyes. The browbones contined up her head, finally forming two large horns that protruded from the back of her skull.

First, two fighters lunged toward Scathar with their swords. They threw them up and at its chest in one motion. Both swords entered the scaly flesh and stuck there, causing Scathar to roar even louder. Fearing for their lives, the fighters hid behind their shields, waiting for its fury. The dragon did not disappoint. It inhaled quickly and spewed out flames onto their waiting shields.

Kieron and Kealy covered their faces from the intense light and heat from the fire.

"It has its fire glands?" Kieron's breathing quicken and his heart felt like it would burst through his chest from excitement and fear. "I've never seen such a ferocious dragon."

But the puny metal shields of the fighters were no match for the intense fire of Scathar. Both fighters became charred bodies in seconds. The scene satiated the crowd's lust for death, and it erupted in great pleasure.

Prince Peter shook his head as he watched the men die before him. Kieron saw the intense anger brimming on the prince's face, but he knew Prince Peter could not lose control. Too much was at stake. Prince Peter turned toward the dragon and took a few deep breaths.

Both Peter and Kieron knew that to defeat Scathar would mean freedom.

"What are they going to do?" Kieron asked Dangler, but he was nowhere to be found. "Where did he go?"

"Dangler?" Kealy searched the area, but only saw other frightened faces on the fighters watching the scene. They looked as though they hoped they weren't next.

Prince Peter and his friend ran behind the other fighters, toward the far side of the arena out of the sight of the dragon as it continued to claw the ground, begging for more challengers. They found a place off to the side.

"Look! The prince is hiding on the other side of the arena," Kieron shouted.

"What should we do now?" Kealy asked.

For a moment, Kieron had no idea what to do, but then he remembered that the battle in the arena was just a distraction. "Come on!" He grabbed Kealy's arm and the two ran past the line of boys and fighters, staring at the giant dragon.

Frightened spectators ran for the caves that exited the prison. Scathar's fire had caused them to panic.

"Where are we going?" Kealy asked once they were alone in the halls carved from stone. A few spectators raced past them. "Should we follow them?"No! To the dragon dungeon. Let's go." Kieron raised his finger to his lips.

Once all the spectators were gone, Kieron motioned for Kealy to follow him. "Shh, we must be quiet."

"The dragon dungeon?" Kealy whispered as she followed Kieron down a darkened hallway.

∽

The dragon dungeon.

Kieron shivered at the thought of returning to the grotesque dungeon where the captive dragons were held between fights or when they were so injured, they were rendered useless. The sounds, the smells, and the sights of those tortured creatures rent his heart in two.

How could he face them again when he had vowed to help them and then disappeared? Kieron rushed down the stone steps with hot blood coursing through his veins. He wanted to set things right and free the dragons so they could have a fighting chance at life.

"What's that awful smell?" Kealy held her hand over her nose.

Kieron paused to prepare her.

"Kealy," he began. "What you're about to see is…well, it's beyond horrific. The smell is just the beginning. There are captive dragons in there. Some have been tortured in the arena. I promise you, the sight will never leave your mind. You'll take it with you, as I have, for the rest of your life."

Kealy's eyes shone with tears.

"But don't let it go to waste. Let this sight fuel your rage toward those who committed such egregious acts of horror on these more intelligent and kind beasts that we have known and enjoyed as friends all our lives." Tears formed in the corners of his eyes as he spoke.

Kealy hugged her friend. "Oh, Kieron," she wept. "I am so glad you are back."

"Ready?" he asked when she parted.

Kealy nodded and the two continued down the stairs.

A vicious roar stopped them.

"Steady," Kieron said. "They are not happy that I have returned, and can probably smell my scent."

They continued to the opening of the cave.

Kealy gasped when she saw the many cages holding dragons of various sizes. Some roared at them while others cowered in the corners out of fear.

"Oh…" Kealy looked away and did her best to hold back the tears.

"No!" Kieron shouted at her. "You must look. Force yourself if you have to, but we owe it to them to look at what's happened to them so we can ensure it never happens again."

Kealy agreed and forced herself to make eye contact with each beast. "I'm so sorry," she mouthed to them.

Some glared at her while others turned away.

"We thought the Dragon Games were noble and adventurous." She cautiously stepped toward the cages. "Never did we think such horror was occurring at your expense."

The dragons snarled at her and rushed the cage wall, ready to pounce. But some tilted their heads as though they understood her words.

"Tell them, Kieron. Tell them how sorry we are."

"Later," he replied as he searched the space. "We don't have much time. Prince Peter is fighting the largest dragon I have ever seen. This is our chance to escape while he distracts the guards, Valbrand, and the crowd."

Kealy wiped her eyes. "Alright. But where is Dangler?I don't know. Help me!" Kieron found a large sword leaning against the wall. He lifted it to try and break the locks on each cage. Kealy rushed over to help him.

Above them, they heard Scathar's ferocious roar echo through several feet of thick rock walls. "Hurry!" Kieron ordered.

Together, they raised the sword high above their heads, then lowered it onto one lock. "Again!" Kieron shouted. The two of them tried many times to break the lock. Finally, they had to rest.

"Are we making any progress at all?" Kealy huffed.

"Yes." Kieron leaned close to inspect the lock. "It's almost broken." He looked at the two dragons inside the cage that the lock secured. They watched with curiosity. "Mythriel ish no ilk even undroth," Kieron told them. The dragons nodded their heads.

"What did you tell them?" Kealy asked.

Kieron turned to her. "You know dragon speak. You need to try it."

She shrugged. "I'm a little rusty."

"I told them that once the cage door is open, to wait for us before flying off." Kieron pointed up to a cave high above them.

"What is that?" Kealy asked.

"That's the entrance the guards use to bring the dragons inside this dungeon. I noticed it the last time I was here." He turned to the dragons and asked them if that was the way out. They each nodded. "You must wait for all to be freed, and we will help the others escape. We'll need you to stop the guards."

"But they've no fire," Kealy reminded him.

Kieron made eye contact with the larger dragon. "Doesn't matter, right?" The dragon's eyes narrowed to mere slits. "He has teeth...they all have teeth and claws that they can use."

"Alright," Kealy said. "Let's try again."

Scathar's roar was heard again, followed by the crowd cheering.Some pebbles fell from the trembling ceiling.

They lifted the sword and lowered it onto the lock, splitting it in two. They cage door swung open, but the dragons inside obediently waited.

"Good," Kieron said. Then he lead Kealy to the next lock, and the next, and the next, until, finally, all the locks were destroyed.

With the healthy, stronger dragons leading the way, they flew up to the cave entrance. Kealy and Kieron helped the weakened dragons out of the cages and to the wall. "Help them!" he ordered the larger dragons. They flew down and used their talons to grab the wings of the weaker dragons, lifting them to the cage opening.

"Now us!" Kieron pointed to himself and Kealy.

The larger dragon flew down and landed beside them.

"Uth vas, an al ish ilién ilerion," Kieron said to the beast. "You are brave and mighty. You deserve to be free. Go, tell the other dragons!"

The dragon lifted its head and stretched its leathery wings. Its dark green scales glistened in the firelight of the torches along the wall.

"Beautiful," Kealy murmured.

She and Kieron climbed onto its back, using the horns to grip on. It took off and flew into the cave. The two youths lowered their heads as it flew through the tunnel, until they spotted the other dragons.

Kieron hopped off, but before Kealy could, he stopped her. "No," he shouted. "You ride this one to tell the other dragons. This one can lead others to freedom. I'll lead the others to where the cages are and free the other dragons."

"How can you do it alone? You don't have the keys to the locks, and you've no sword to use this time."

Kieron patted the neck of another large dragon. "With these claws, I don't need another sword or the keys. Right?"

The dragon snarled, revealing its sharp teeth. It dragged its talons in the dirt. Each was several inches long.

"Yes." Kealy gulped. "I see what you mean."

Kieron grinned.

"What do you want us to do?" she asked.

"Meet me back here for the signal." Kieron walked away with three dragons following him.

"What's the signal?" she shouted after him.

"You'll know it when you see it."

CHAPTER 10

The roar of the crowd grew louder as they approached one cave that opened up to the Great Arena. Kieron hunched over and scurried to the entrance of the cave. He motioned for the dragons to stand back, out of sight. They snorted and clawed at the ground, but they obeyed and did their best to hide their large bodies and wings.

When he peeked out, he could see Valbrand's cave across from him. It was filled with Valbrand's friends, celebrating and cheering, but he could not see the warden. That was a good thing.

Below, Kieron watched Prince Peter battle Valbrand's dragon.

Together, Prince Peter and his friend ran to where four other fighters faced the dragon. The cheers from the spectators were so loud, Kieron covered his ears. Prince Peter gazed up to see Valbrand standing with his arms crossed in front of his chest. Peter held his shield and sword tightly, waiting for Scathar to make its move. It studied each fighter as they took position. Then, the familiar hissing started.

"Oh no," Kieron said. He knew the warning sound of oncoming dragon fire when he heard it.

The fighters on the arena floor hid behind their shields, but Peter and Jason ran behind the dragon's body while it sent flames shooting forward.

Prince Peter climbed onto its back and plunged his sword deep into the dragon's spine several times. It flapped the wings, hitting Peter and catapulting him to the ground with a hard thud.

Kieron gasped.

Prince Peter did not move at first, but then he turned and reached for his shield.

The dragon scale. Kieron's eyes widened as he watched the scene.

The dragon inhaled quickly in order to burn him alive. Sensing this, the other fighter raised his sword high and brought it down onto the dragon's tail with such force that he sliced off the tip. Blood sprayed everywhere. The crowd that didn't run for their lives applauded and stomped their feet.

Kieron watched them in amazement. "That dragon could burn them all to ashes," he said to no one in particular. "If they knew what was good for them, they'd get out of here."

Scathar hissed. The other fighters who stood watching suddenly left the sidelines and joined in the fight, sensing a chance to attack the dragon. One fighter threw his sword, penetrating the dragon's chest. But the dragon ignored him as it pivoted to find Prince Peter.

Their eyes met.

Peter and Valbrand's dragon, Scathar, stood mesmerized. Scathar's pupils were black vertical slits inside the glowing red eyes. It panted, revealing many long teeth the size of swords.

Another fighter climbed onto its back and began to stab it ferociously, but the dragon did not take its gaze off of Peter. It seemed to recognize him.

"Oh no." Kieron turned to the dragons, hiding in the shadows. "Valbrand's dragon is going to burn Prince Peter."

One dragon squawked.

"Talk to it?" Kieron turned to watch Scathar again. "I don't think so. Something tells me that dragon speaks dragonspeak."

Scathar took a few steps forward and inhaled. Peter bent down and hid behind the scale of the Great Dragon in time to meet the force of the flames hitting him and sending him falling backward. He leaned forward, gaining his footing again. The intense heat was almost more than he could bear, but the shield held fast.

"It worked!" Kieron shouted. He turned to the dragons.He could see their tails swish from side to side. "The Dragon's scale held fast. The prince is winning. It is almost time for us to make our escape."

Kieron turned to watch the scene below. In the corner of his eye, he saw guards holding the reins of several dragons near the large entrance to the arena.

"Look!" He pointed to where the guards stood. Then he ran over to the many dragons hiding with him. "I need you to fly over there and speak to those dragons." He motioned for them to follow him to the ledge.

As they did, Kieron checked to see if Valbrand had noticed, but he was too involved in the battle below.

"See those dragons? Un vas eth lorien il mythrién. Il nuriel mythrién." Kieron ordered them to fly over and speak to the dragons.

But they hesitated, so he climbed on top of one and nudged it off the ledge. "This way!"

As they flew off the ledge, several more dragons followed.

Kieron knew Valbrand was probably watching them now. But as soon as they faced the guards holding the dragons, Kieron spoke dragonspeak to them.

"Is iliel! Us vath bethiel even ish iliel!" He shouted to them to follow him to freedom.

Confused, the dragons stood watching, but the guards ran to get some bows and arrows.

"Uh oh!" Kieron nudged his dragon to take off, but it continued to hover. "What are you doing? Let's go!"

But the beast flapped its wings. The guards ran toward them and loaded their bows with arrows. "Come on! We must fly away."

But his dragon roared loudly, startling the other dragons on the ground. To his amazement, Kieron saw all them spread their wings and take flight just as the guards released their arrows.

"Yes!" he shouted as they flew back to the cave. "It worked! They understood us."

Once they landed on the ledge, Kieron hopped off and looked at each one. "You all must go now and speak to the other dragons inside here. You know where they are and I don't. You know what to tell them. They must all fly to freedom now."

Scathar's roar interrupted him. Kieron turned and noticed Valbrand pointing at him and ordering his guards to get him.

"We've not much time. Once this battle is over, Prince Peter is going to free the slaves."

But the dragons turned to one another in confusion.

"Sorry, I forgot you can't understand everything I'm saying." Kieron thought for a second. "Uthviel, ish va?"

The dragons nodded their heads.

"Aye, uthvas norien. Norien ish ilriéll." He pointed to the arena. "Scathar myth valien. Bethud an anath nathra!"

One by one, the dragons nodded, spread their wings, and took off.

"Yes! Nathra mish draco!" Kieron shouted as he watched them fly off to find more dragons. "You can do it!"

Below, Valbrand's dragon tilted its head, as though amazed that the shield in Prince Peter's hands did not yield. It inhaled again, and more fire spewed forth, hitting Peter again. Kieron watched as Peter leaned into it with great strength. The dragon came forward and sniffed the shield as it smoldered from the heat. Raising its head, Scathar whipped its body around, sending the men on its back flying to the ground.

In anger, Scathar stomped on the motionless bodies of the fighters to the approval of the crowd.

Kieron turned away, sickened by the sight.

Only three fighters remained alive.

Instead of attacking the dragon, one fighter suspiciously lunged toward Prince Peter.

"What's this?" Kieron shouted.

The fighter hit Prince Peter with his entire body, sending him to the ground. The Dragon scale shield flew from his arm.

"Oh no!" Kieron said.

Then fighter stood over the prince, raising his sword high above Peter's body. Peter rolled out of the way in time for the sword to pierce the ground. Peter rolled again and retrieved his shield. Scathar roared when it noticed Peter.

"Look out!" Kieron shouted.

The dragon, with swords protruding from its bleeding body, did not lose a step. It appeared to be stronger than all the other dragons that had fought in the arena. It dug at the ground, challenging the fighters to charge. The crowd chanted its name again and again.

"Scathar! Scathar!" they shouted.

The one fighter grabbed his sword and came at Peter again.Peter blocked his attacks with the Dragon scale shield over and over until he used it to hit the fighter across the neck. Kieron saw that it was Damon who had fought in the arena before.

Damon fell back, unable to breath for a moment. Peter grabbed his sword and came at the fighter, but was met with the sword again.

Damon came at Peter, who used his shield again to block the blows until the shield flew out of Peter's hands. The two swung their swords at each other. Peter sliced the exposed flesh on the Damon's shoulder. He screamed and grabbed the wound. After staring at his own blood, he lunged toward Peter, who met the sword with his own. Peter struck him down again.

"He's winning!" Kieron shouted.

Scathar made its move toward Peter, but the prince saw it approaching. He pushed Damon back, then ran to retrieve the Dragon scale shield. The dragon swiftly approached the fighter.

"Look behind you!" Peter warned Damon.

But Kieron could see that Damon had ignored the prince's warning and ran to retrieve something on the ground.

"Leave it!" Peter yelled.

Scathar seemed relentless. Valbrand's dragon wanted Peter at all costs.

With rage, Damon came at the prince, who blocked him and pushed him back. He fell to the ground. Just then, Peter could hear Scathar inhale.

They all could hear it.

"Protect yourself!" Kieron shouted to the prince.

"Get behind my shield, you idiot!" Peter shouted to Damon.

But he rose and came at Peter again with fierce hatred in his eyes.

It was no use. Just as Damon ran at Peter with his sword, Scathar spewed forth enough fire to engulf Damon in flames. Peter hid behind his shield just in time.

From high above the arena floor, Kieron could hear the tormented screams of Damon as the flames hit his unprotected body. When the flames ceased, Prince Peter peeked over the Dragon scale shield and saw the charred remains of his opponent.

In horror, Kieron watched as Scathar turned its attention to the prince. *If he is killed, the kingdom of Illiath will be without a ruler.* Kieron swallowed back his fear *And our plan of escape is destroyed.*

"I've got to do something!" He ran through the tunnel.

∽

The dark, musty tunnel seemed to go on forever, but Kieron trusted his gut feeling that he was headed in the right direction.

When he spotted a torch in a sconce, he grabbed it and made his way further down the tunnel, where he ran into more of the freed dragons, confused and wandering in the hallways.

"This way," he commanded the dragons he had freed from the dungeon. One roared, causing him to pause and answer its question in dragonspeak. "We are going to Dangler's quarters. We should let him know that we are here and ready to fight for escape," Kieron said in its language.

But the larger dragon grumbled to him in its language. It's red-tinted scales and violet eyes made it stand out from the other darker dragons. When he translated the dragonspeak, Kieron's face drained of all blood. "What?" His skin shivered.

The dragons explained in dragonspeak that Dangler was last seen packing up what little he could before escaping. For Lord Bedlam had entered the prison and was coming for him.

The idea that the dark lord roamed the halls, searching out his enemies, made Kieron freeze in place.

But the weakest dragon nudged him with its snout, urging him to continue. He turned to the frail dragon, running his hand over its course scales. Kieron could feel the deep scars from where the beast had been beaten and wounded while in captivity. He wondered what peaceful life it once had outside the walls. Or perhaps it had been born in captivity, never knowing the joy of flying free, over the White Forest or the green hills of Glouslow. Perhaps none of the dragons with him had ever flown near the glistening castle of Vulgaard, built of diamonds mined from the Ranvieg Mountains long ago. Kieron closed his eyes, remembering the magnificent structure sparkling in the sunlight. When he opened his eyes, he swallowed back the tears that began to form in his eyes. *No*, he thought. *I won't shed any more tears for the past. Instead, we will fight for the future of Vulgaard.*

He patted the dragon's head gently. "You're right. We cannot quit now. I won't quit on you. I made a promise, and I intend to keep that promise."

Before he took a step forward, Kieron heard some approaching footsteps. "Shh," he ordered the dragons. All of them stood completely still, which is hard for dragons to do. The Dracos stepped

"Escaping the Prison"

on the wings of the Wyverns who snapped at the Dracos.

"Shush!" Kieron ordered. "You don't want to return to the dungeons, do you?"

The dragons stopped fiddling.

Around the corner, firelight was seen, illuminating the cave walls. *Guards,* Kieron thought. *This is it. We've been caught.* He frowned and then reached down to pick up a large rock, hoping he could hit one guard and bide the dragons some time to escape.

One dragon growled a throaty ominous growl, causing the person holding the torch to stop. More dragons growled.

Kieron took advantage of the pause and crept toward the torchlight, peeking around the corner. "Kealy!" he cried.

She almost dropped the torch from fright. Kealy ran to her friend and spotted the dragons, hunched together in the cave tunnel.

"Kieron!" she cried into his shoulder. "I'm so glad to see you again."

"What are you doing here? I told you to wait!" He parted from her embrace.

"I waited for as long as I could, but I heard more roars from the crowd and then I heard some screaming coming from the tunnels all around us. So I made an escape." She pointed to the dragons behind her. "With these fellows."

Kieron's eyes widened when he saw three more dragons with his friend. They each blinked as their eyes tried to adjust to the torchlight.

"These poor dragons. We've got to get them out." Kieron shook his head.

"Kieron…" Kealy's face contorted as though in pain. "Um, about Dangler."

"What is it?" Kieron leaned in. "Is he alright?"

"Well…" Kealy fiddled with her hands. "You see…"

The thunderous roar from the crowd below interrupted Kealy. Kieron ran to the edge of the cave, overlooking the arena below. There he saw two dragons facing each other. One was Scathar, but he other was even more ferocious. It towered over Valbrand's dragon. The people in the stands fled for their lives.

"What is it?" Kealy asked.

Kieron turned to her. "The signal, that's what it is. Time for us to get out of here!"

Together, they ran down the corridor toward Dangler's quarters.

"But he's not there!" Kealy shouted after Kieron.

"What do you mean he's not there?" he replied while he ran.

"I mean he fled," Kealy huffed.

The dragons roared when Kealy said this. Kieron slid to a stop. Behind them, they could still hear the roars of the two dragons, battling in the arena.

"He fled?" Kieron thought about the idea of escaping without the help of his friend, the Dragon Master.

"It's okay. We have the dragons. We can escape through the tunnels we used to enter this dreaded place." Kealy pointed upward to a few caves above them.

One of the smaller dragons took flight and entered one cave.

"Follow that dragon!" Kieron hopped onto the back of one dragon and nudged it to take flight. Kealy did the same.

All of the dragons obeyed and flew into the caves with precision.

All but one.

The weak dragon squawked from below. Kieron heard it and stopped his dragon by pulling on its horns, but the desperate beast would not stop. Kieron hopped off and tumbled onto the damp ground, watching all the dragons make their way through the darkened tunnel. He couldn't blame them for not stopping to help. They were desperate to finally be set free.

Kieron returned to where the tunnel opened up near Dangler's quarters and spotted the frail dragon attempting to fly. But her wings were too damaged to take flight.

"We'll have to get you out another way." He told her. Kieron hopped down and patted the saddened dragon on her head. She nuzzled his shoulder. Her smooth scales were a light gray, almost white. "It will be alright. I will not leave you. Understand?" He looked into her large shiny eyes. "I think I will call you Fawn, because you remind me of a little fawn I saw in the forest once. Come, now, Fawn, let's see where this tunnel leads to."

As Kieron took a step, he heard a ruckus from the tunnel he had just left. Both he and Fawn glanced upward and saw Vâken peek his head out.

"Vâken!" Kieron tried to climb the rock wall, but his loyal

dragon flew down and scooped him up onto his back. "No! Stop!"

Kieron tugged onto his dragon's horns and he stopped flapping his wings. Kieron pointed to Fawn and her damaged wings. "I can't leave it here."

Vâken snorted and squawked in dragon language to Fawn. The frail dragon perked up and nodded.

"You mean, you can help her get up there?" Kieron pointed up the slick rock wall. "Are you sure?"

Before he could think about it, Vâken flew Kieron up and into the tunnel, where he hopped off and watched as his faithful dragon returned to Fawn. The poor dragon was so weak she could barely stand, so she leaned against the wall and waited. Vâken scooped her up and was about to take flight when the shouts of men could be heard coming from the darkened hallway behind the two dragons.

"Hurry!" Kieron shouted.

Several guards ran toward the two stranded dragons and held their torches high. Fawn did her best to roar and Vâken flapped his wings, but the guards laughed at the two beasts before them.

One guard approached with chains. "Grab that smaller one and I'll chain it. Together, we'll haul it back to the cages."

Kieron's eyes grew large and his anger boiled within him when he heard those words and saw the men approaching the dragons. He lurched forward to jump onto the men when Kealy grabbed his arm. He jerked toward her.

She shook her head "no" and pointed at Vâken. "Remember," she whispered. "Vâken can still spew fire."

The corners of Kieron's mouth slowly rose into a grin. Together, they returned to the ledge to watch the scene.

The guards lifted the chains and stepped toward Fawn. Vâken snarled, inhaled, and made that familiar hissing sound that Kieron knew too well.

"What?" the guard said. "I thought these dragons had their fire glands re—"

But before he could finish his sentence, a thin stream of fire shot forth from Vâken's snout, hitting the guards. They screamed and ran from the area.

"Yes!" Kieron shouted to his dragon below. "Now see if you can get both of you up here."

Vâken motioned for Fawn to grip onto his back, and then he

flew them both into the cave where Kieron and Kealy waited.

"Where are the other dragons?" he asked her.

"Gone! This tunnel opens to the mountain precipice near the cave where we left our dragons behind, remember?

Kieron exhaled. "That seems like a million years ago."

"True." Kealy shoved him. "Once all the dragons saw the wide open space, they took off. It was a glorious sight to see." Kealy ran alongside Kieron.

∽

Standing on the mountain precipice, Kieron breathed in the fresh cold air. The sun was low behind the mountains, and night was soon approaching. He patted Vâken on the head. "You did well, my friend."

They stood watching all the freed dragons fly away. Some headed toward the sea while others flew toward the plains.

"No matter where they go, they'll be free." Kieron sighed.

"Now what do we do?" Kealy asked.

"You and I head back and free more dragons." Kieron started to turn around to head back into the prison when he heard dragons growling. "Look!"

He pointed to several young and lithe dragons flying toward them. "Get out of the way!" he shouted to Kealy. She leapt to her right as the dragons flew past her.

"Whoa," she said as she watched them fly off. One after the other shot out of the cave and into freedom. "What a sight."

"It must be over," Kieron said to her. "Prince Peter must have won. The dragons and all the slaves must be free now."

"Let's get out of here and head home." Kealy hopped onto Vâken's back and motioned for Kieron to join her.

"But Fawn," Kieron said. He hugged the frail dragon's neck. "She's too weak to fly off this mountainside."

But the little dragon flapped her wings, surprising Kieron.

"Looks like she's willing to try." Kealy smiled.

Kieron took her head into his hands and stared into her wide eyes. "You just glide down, okay? Glide to that meadow over there. You'll be able to land in the soft grass." He smiled. "Uth vas mythrién ish il eleøn."

The dragon nuzzled his chest, then stepped to the edge and took off. Kieron, Kealy, and Vâken watched the little dragon glide through the cool mountain air. Although Fawn's wings were damaged, the will to live in freedom proved to be enough to get her to the meadow.

"Look at her go," Kealy said in a soft voice. "I can only imagine the joy she's feeling."

Together, they watched the little dragon glide to a safe landing in the meadow.

"She'll be safe there. I'm sure other dragons will find her and she'll make a home." Kieron hopped onto Vâken, behind Kealy.

"Maybe one day, the dragons can safely return to these mountain caves dragons once called home for millennium." Kealy took hold of Vâken's horns. "Ready, boy?"

Vâken stepped to the ledge, then dove off the cliff, heading down the mountainside like a comet Kieron once saw shooting through the night's sky.

At just the right time, Vâken pulled up and flapped his wings, joining other dragons already in flight.

"Look at all of them!" Kieron shouted.

Beside them flew Wyverns and Dracos that once were imprisoned inside the dreaded prison.

As they flew around the mountain, Kieron spotted Kealy's dragon, Söen. "Over there, Kealy." He motioned toward his left.

When she spotted her beloved dragon, she waved. Vâken landed in the tall grass and Kealy hopped off. Running toward her small dragon, she yelped with joy.

"I didn't think I'd ever see you again," she said as she embraced her neck.

Vâken panted, exhausted from the escape from Rünbrior Prison. To help it rest, Kieron dismounted and tried to find some wet grass. "Hold on, boy," he said. "I'll find you some—"

A leather water pouch landed at his feet, interrupting his sentence.

"Hey," Kieron said. He bent over to pick it up. "Where did this come from?" As he looked up, his eyes met those of his brother, Théan.

Kieron stepped back, convinced he was looking at a ghost.

"It's me, little brother." Théan held out his hand. "Your dragon looks thirsty."

Kieron dropped the water pouch and ran to his older brother, almost knocking him down with his embrace. Théan squeezed Kieron tightly.

"It's alright," he whispered."It's alright."

"I thought…" Kieron wept. "I thought you were dead."

"Me, too." Théan laughed.

When they parted, Théan messed up Kieron's hair. "I thought for sure you were probably dead, too. Imagine my surprise to see you here again."

"But how? How did you escape?" Kieron asked.

"Once they took you away, I woke up and untied Mom and Dad. Everleigh and the others remained hidden in the back of the house. They were never seen by the thugs."

Kieron exhaled once he learned his parents and siblings were safe.

"What a nice surprise." Kealy stood with her hands on her hips.

Kieron wiped the tears from his eyes. "And Mom and Dad? Where are they now?"

"They're okay." Théan turned toward the forest. "We all escaped to the woods by the pond. We built a shelter to wait it out. Dad, Mythiel, and I hunted and fished. Mom and the girls cooked the meals. We've been eagerly awaiting any news. The rumor is that this is the end for Valbrand and his prison."

"It's no rumor." Kieron stood by Vâken. "My dragon and others all helped us escape. He's not so worthless after all."

Théan grinned and made his way over to Kieron's dragon. "No, he is not. No dragon is worthless. I have come to learn just how important they all are. In fact, it is good that you both made it out. We've been waiting for the sign. And, tonight we have it. We watched as all the dragons shot out of the caves and flew away to freedom. Some landed here, eager to join us in the fight. They, too, have lost so much and now seek vengeance. Get your dragons some water. We've no time to rest."

"What?" Kealy turned toward the sunset. "What do you mean?"

"Unfortunately, the Riders of Rünbrior do not give up that easily. The queen has sent her Dragon Riders to fight them off. Get ready. The battle's just beginning." Théan turned and walked off toward his waiting dragon. Behind him were several elfin men, sitting atop their dragons.

"Battle?" Kealy searched the skies. Far off into the sunset, she spotted them. "Uh oh."

Kieron turned toward her. "What is it?"

"The Riders of Rünbrior." She took off toward Söen, mounted the dragon, then flew off.

"But, we have no weapons!" Kieron shouted after her.

"Here." Théan sat atop his dragon, hovering over Kieron. Pegasus flapped his mighty wings, looking more powerful than ever to Kieron, after having worked with all the thin sickly dragons within the prison. Théan dropped a bow and quiver of arrows onto the ground at Kieron's feet. Next came a small sword. "These will do. I'll make sure Kealy has a sword."

Kieron grabbed his bow and arrows, then watched as Théan flew toward Kealy.

"Can this really be happening?" Kieron asked his dragon. It munched on some moist grass. "Here's some water. You'd better take a sip now, because who knows how long it will be before we both get another chance."

When Vâken had his fill, Kieron gulped down some water. He tossed aside the water pouch and grabbed the small sword, twisting it in his hand. The thin, dull blade lacked luster, and the leather straps that wrapped the grip were worn. But Kieron knew he'd make it work.

"Come on, Vâken," he said, taking hold of the horns. Staying atop the dragon would be difficult without a saddle and reins, but he knew he'd have to do his best to save the kingdom. He leaned close and whispered to the dragon. "This is it, boy. The real Dragon Games. Except we're not battling to win a tournament. This time, we're fighting to save Glouslow, the White Forest, and Vulgaard. Our homes, our way of life...everything we hold dear to us." Kieron's parents and siblings came to mind. "So we'll have to win this one."

He climbed atop Vâken's back.

"All that training we did this summer? We'll have to make good use of it." Kieron took one last look around at the land that was his home. "Ready?"

He and Vâken took off into the air to join his brother and Kealy.

CHAPTER 11

O nce in the air, Kieron had a better picture of the build-up to battle. His eyes grew large when he spotted his friends hovering over the area where men and elves on horses waited. The other dragon riders flew back and forth around the mountain.

"Aerin!" Kieron nudged his dragon over to where his friends sat atop their dragons. "What are you doing here?"

"Kieron!" Thyler flew over to him atop Fly.

"How…where…when?" Kieron struggled to ask his questions. "What happened?"

"What was the signal?" Kealy shouted to Thyler.

"The White Owl turned into its true form, the Dragon of the Forest!" he shouted over the wind.

Kieron's mouth dropped. "*The* Dragon of the Forest?"

Thyler nodded. "It appeared inside the Great Arena, helping Prince Peter escape." Thyler pointed to three young people, sitting atop their dragons. "Those are Prince Peter's friends. They came from Illiath to join with Prince Thætil and the others."

Kieron turned in the saddle to see how far back the line of troops went. He saw elves, men, and dwarves all the way to the river. "This is really happening." A wide smile came to his face.

Rocks fell from the mountain to the ridge below. The earth shook and frightened the men and their horses. Kieron saw a tunnel in the mountain and heeled Vâken's side to fly over to it. Once they landed, he hopped off and led Vâken by the reins near the tunnel.

"Kieron, what are you doing?" Kealy asked as she landed her dragon.

"I can't wait. I have to see what's happening. I'll find Dangler. He'll tell me everything." Kieron waved to her. "Follow me if you want."

Thyler, Aerin and the others landed in the cave as well. "What's going on?" Thyler asked.

Kealy crept to the mouth of the tunnel and tugged on Söen's reins for her to follow. "Come along if you want," she said to Thyler and the others.

Thyler hopped off his dragon and turned to the others. "What do you want to do?"

Aerin shrugged.

Kealy rolled her eyes as she followed Kieron. "I think we should stay right here, all safe and sound. Now look at you." She glared at Kieron. "I guess I'll have to save you yet again."

Kieron turned around. "Save me?" He laughed. "Ha! You didn't save me."

The boys stayed near the mouth of the cave for a few more minutes, thinking about it.

"I don't want to go back inside that prison again," Aerin shouted after Kieron.

Thyler smirked. "Well, I don't want to hang around here. Either we head back to the battlefield below, or we follow after Kieron to see where Dangler is." He turned to the others. "Well?"

Yon whined. "Aww…couldn't we just go home like we had planned?"

"You can!" Kieron shouted from the cave. "But I'm going after Dangler. I want to see what happened to him." Kieron and Kealy disappeared into the tunnel.

"Kieron, wait up," cried Kealy.

"Shh," he whispered. "Up ahead."

They navigated through the familiar tunnel, passing by bones scattered on the ground. They could hear a commotion ahead. When the tunnel ended, they could see light from fires burning and the sound of men's voices shouting orders. The roar of a large dragon was so loud, they had to cover their ears.

"What was that?" Kealy whispered.

"One large dragon, that's for sure." Kieron looked around.

Suddenly, he saw Dangler rush by.

"Dangler!" Kieron shouted.

The old man stopped and looked around the space.

"Up here!" Kieron waved.

Dangler looked up and his eyes widened when he saw the elfin boy. "What are you doing here?" he shouted. "Get back! Get back in there and go home, boy."

But Kieron started to climb down the wall instead. Dangler raced over to him.

"Stop! Get back up there!" Dangler shouted.

Kieron hopped down and scooted behind a stack of spears. "What's happening? Did Prince Peter win in the arena?"

Dangler covered his eyes as though frustrated. "Do you know what I had to go through to get you and those other boys out of here? Do you?"

Kieron shrugged.

"You need to get out of here. It's too dangerous to be in here. Go back."

Another dragon roar shook the ground.

"The dragons are free. We are finally free. I wanted to make sure you are, too," Kieron said.

Dangler grabbed his shoulders and stared intently into his eyes. "Kieron. Listen to me. This isn't a game. Lord Bedlam is coming. He's angry with Valbrand for putting the prince in the arena. He's angry at me for helping the prince. You need to get as far away from this mountain as you can. Do you understand?"

Kieron nodded.

"Kieron, what's happening?" Kealy asked from above.

Dangler glanced up and Kealy peeking over the ledge.

"You didn't bring all them back here, did you?" He returned his glance to Kieron. "You foolish boy. You've put all of them in grave danger. I don't think any of you understand what's happening. It is the battle between good and absolute evil. A battle that has had to happen for thousands of years, and it's happening now. You are all in the middle of it. Lord Bedlam doesn't care that you are children. He will kill you all, without hesitation. Now get back up there." He dragged Kieron by the arm. "Go on. Now!"

"But I—"

"Just go!" Dangler started to help Kieron up the wall when a second dragon roar happened, followed by screams from the people trapped in the mountain.

"Oh no," Dangler said. His eyes filled with fear. "It's too late."

Men began streaming into the space, knocking over stacks of swords and shields as they ran by. The looks of horror on their faces told Kieron everything he needed to know. What was happening in that arena was not supposed to happen.

"It's too late. Run! All of you, run away." Dangler backed away. "I've got to go."

"Dangler!" Kieron shouted at his friend's back, but it was no use. Dangler ran off into the darkness.

"Climb up. We've got to get out of here now." Kealy stretched out her hand and helped Kieron climb back up the wall to the ledge.

"You're right. Let's get out of here. Valbrand must have set loose his guards and dragons."

The screams of more people tryingto escape were heard below.

Kieron and Kealy raced through the darkened tunnel, stumbling over stones and rocks until they made it to the opening.

"Vâken!" Kieron shouted to his dragon. He bent down so Kieron could mount his back, and away they flew off the ledge of the cave. All of his friends followed and turned back to see a sight they thought they'd never see.

Hundreds of dragons of all sizes shot out of the various caves of the mountain. Kieron grinned. "They're free." He started laughing as Vâken glided through the air.

"Look at that!" Kealy shouted. Kieron whooped and hollered at the sight.

"They're finally free!" Aerin shouted.

"Yeah, but…" Thyler pointed to the dragons. "They don't look too pleased about being set free."

"They're coming this way!" Aerin swerved his dragon out of the way of the angry beasts.

"Watch out!" Kieron nudged Vâken to dive away from the angry dragons, but it caught the attention of one. It swooped down and spewed a line of fire at them, nicking Vâken's tail. It roared and turned around to spew its flame of vengeance. Kieron held on tightly to keep from falling off its back. "Whoa!" he cried. "Warn me next time."

When Vâken straightened out, the angry dragon caught up to Vâken again and opened its mouth to fire at it. Vâken dove down close to the ground, and then swerved upwards. The motion made

Kieron's innards rise up within him. His face turned green.

Vâken spun around near the trees, but the angry dragon stayed close behind it. Kieron turned to shout at it. "Why are you angry at us? We helped free you!"

The dragon's eyes glowed red with anger.

"Uthvas ul orien! Ishba thul il olrien! Nathran!" Kieron spoke dragonspeak, hoping it would understand. The dragon's countenance softened a bit. Kieron pulled on the reins to slow Vâken down. The angry dragon flew beside them. "We helped save you from that awful place. You should be angry at them. Nulien thriel nos uthrien!" Kieon pointed to the prison guards being captured below by the many elfin guards. "Not us."

The dragon snorted and flew away. Vâken and Kieron joined the others. Many other angry dragons attacked his friends.

Aerin's dragon spun around so fast, the boy could barely hold on. Kieron and Vâken made it over to him and shouted at the angry dragon in dragonspeak.

It jerked around to see who was speaking to it, and Kieron realized it understood every word he said. He motioned for it to slow down and it did.

Aerin's dragon stopped spinning, but the boy looked sick to his stomach.

"You'd better land," Kieron told Aerin's dragon and it obeyed. Next, he spotted Thyler in trouble.

"Vâken, let's go help Thyler!" Together, they shot through the air, behind the dragon chasing after Thyler.

"Help!" he cried as his dragon swerved left and right to avoid the spurts of fire coming from the angry dragon behind them.

Kieron shouted in three different dragon dialects, but the beast continued on its path to burn Thyler out of the sky. "Stop! We're the ones who helped free you."

But the dragon never relented. It seethed with anger, and in its eyes, Kieron could see it wouldn't be satisfied until it had its revenge.

Vâken beat its wings as fast as it could to catch up, but the angry dragon was too quick. It spurt out short bursts of flames at Thyler's dragon, barely missing it each time. It continued to swerve out of the way, but Kieron knew the angry dragon would soon predict Thyler's dragon's moves.

Vâken flew underneath the angry beast, so close that Kieron could touch it. He had an arrow but didn't want to kill it, so he punched it in the belly, causing it to pull back. But now it was behind Vâken, ready to spew fire. Kieron pulled up on the reins and Vâken shot straight up, spinning around as fast as it could. Then it hovered in the air for a second before free-falling down to the earth like a falcon.

Kieron leaned forward, gripping Vâken's neck and holding his breath. He tried to see if the angry dragon had followed them, but the force of the wind was too strong. He couldn't move until Vâken pulled up.

With seconds to spare, it pulled up and headed into the woods. "Uh oh," Kieron muttered. He closed his eyes and buried his head behind the small horns along Vâken's neck, hoping low-lying tree branches wouldn't strike him and knock him off his back. "Keep going, boy."

Vâken obeyed and zig-zagged successfully through the trees, easily navigating them. An idea popped into Kieron's head. As they approached a tree, he turned to see the angry dragon close behind. Kieron reached out and grabbed a branch and then released it in time for it to hit the angry dragon, sending it spiraling out of control, eventually landing in a pond.

"Pull up, Vâken!" Kieron ordered. His dragon did so and glided on the breeze, resting for a bit. "Be prepared for an even angrier dragon to come out of the trees," he warned Vâken. Kieron removed an arrow from the quiver and loaded his bow, ready to defend his little dragon.

Sure enough, the angry dragon appeared above the tree tops, facing Kieron and Vâken. Its red eyes glowed, and smoke rose from its nostrils. Water dripped from its wings, making it hard for it to stay in flight. Kieron pulled back the arrow, ready to release it.

"I don't want to, but I will," he shouted to the beast. "Please, don't make me shoot you. Uth vas beckan iliuth. Mythrien!"

The dragon flapped its wings and listened to Kieron.

"We helped free you from that horrid place. Now you are free. Go fly to your home. Please!"

The dragon turned and flew away.

Kieron lowered his bow and exhaled. "Come on, Vâken. Let's go join the others." Together, they landed on a grassy hill as the sunset. Kieron patted his little dragon on its head. Vâken panted from exhaustion, but snuggled up to him, resting his brow on Kieron's chest. "Awww, thank you, friend. You did some amazing flying up there. I'm so proud of you."

"Kieron!" Thyler shouted as he ran toward his friend. "Thank you."

They shook hands. "Glad I could help. Have all the other dragons flown away?"

"Yes. But look there." Thyler pointed to an assembly of escaped prisoners approaching the famous commander of King Alexander's troops, General Aluein.

"Is that…General Aluein?" Kieron's eyes widened.

"The banner of Illiath follows after him, so I believe it is." Thyler pointed to the banner, flapping in the breeze.

A rumbling came from Ranvieg Mountains as giant boulders came tumbling down.

"What's happening?" Kieron asked. "Are those prisoners?" He pointed to a gathering of boys and young men, waiting in the grass. "Did they escape?"

"That's what we were told," said Aerin.

Kealy ran up to meet Kieron. "That's Prince Peter there with General Aluein."

Kieron craned his neck to see the famous Prince of Illiath.

"He's introducing Prince Thætil and Prince Thurdin to the general." Kealy's voice was loud with excitement.

A chill ran over Kieron's skin, making him rub his bare arms. "This is exciting."

"Kieron!" Théan shouted for his brother.

With a wide smile, Kieron ran to meet him.

"The dragons and all the prisoners are free," Théan said as he approached. "But the battle has just begun."

"What do you mean, Théan?" Kieron asked.

"I mean that soon Valbrand's guards will make one last attempt to fight. And we will be ready for them. Mount up!"

Kieron turned and spotted hundreds of elves from Glouslow and nearby counties approaching from behind Théan. Many marched on foot carrying swords, while others flew on dragons.

Kieron smiled at the sight of his countrymen and women, willing to defend the land and kingdom of Vulgaard. His heart raced

"Théan"

within him, sending a rush of joy through his body.

"Absolutely!" Kieron raised his arm into the air. "Let's go!"

He and his friends ran to their dragons and hopped on for more action.

"Wait." Théan said. "But first…"

"What?" Kieron asked.

"I need to get you back home to Mother and Father." He patted Kieron's back.

"No, not yet. I want to partake in this battle." Kieron watched his brother climb atop his dragon.

"I promised them. I have to keep my promise. After that, you can make your choice." Théan took off into the sky and waited for Kieron to follow.

"No," Kieron insisted. "I cannot return home again."

"Let's go," Théan replied with a stern look.

Kieron frowned. "Théan, you and I both know the truth."

"What are you talking about? Come on. Let's go. We've not much time before the battle begins." Théan took hold of the reins.

Kieron pursed his lips. "Listen to me!"

Théan froze.

"I will not return home again." Kieron stared at his older brother. "Ever."

Hopping off his dragon, Théan approached Kieron.

"You and I both know Father blames me for Aislinn's death," Kieron explained. "And I cannot go home to face his wrath and anger ever again."

Before Théan could respond, Kieron and Vâken took off into the air. From above, Kieron could see all the freed prisoners falling to the ground and rolling in the green grass, rejoicing. Some hugged each other and hopped up and down. He saw Prince Peter shake hands with Prince Thætil of Vulgaard. As he nudged his dragon to follow the other dragon riders, a large object blocked out the sun for a moment. Kieron jerked around to see a sight he never thought he'd live to see. His jaw dropped and his eyes widened.

Gliding across the sky was the largest, most majestic dragon Kieron had ever seen. It's glass-like scales glistened in the sun, making it seem almost like an apparition.

But it was real.

"It's the Dragon of the Forest, Kieron!" Théan shouted. The Great Dragon's massive wings flapped, and the beast rose higher into the air. The freed prisoners on the ground whooped and hollered at it. The Dragon dove close to the ground, and Kieron saw Prince Peter wave to it as it transformed into the White Owl. It landed onto the prince's extended arm.

"Did you see that?" Kieron shouted to his brother.

Théan laughed. "Yes! We have the Great Dragon on our side, Kieron."

The brothers flew off to face Valbrand's guards in the sky.

CHAPTER 12

T he violet late afternoon sky provided the perfect background for the last desperate attempt of Valbrand's guards to capture the slaves and dragons.

Violet hues represented peace and hope to Kieron.

He and Kealy nodded toward each other, removed arrows, and loaded their bows as several guards approached on black dragons.

The irony was more than apparent. To keep the peace and hope, violence and blood would have to stain the peaceful land below. There was no other way.

"For the dragons!" Kieron shouted. He nudged Vâken forward, and the two shot through the sky.

Kieron pulled back on the bow string and took aim at a guard. His grotesque face, twisted with rage, contrasted perfectly with the soft sky. "Die, elfin scum!"

"Not today," Kieron said as he released his arrow. It pierced the guard's left arm, making him scream and turn his dragon to the left. It spiraled downward, sending its rider to the ground.

Kieron winced at the sight of the dead guard's lifeless body. He gulped. *Is violence and death the only way?* He hesitantly loaded his bow again, taking aim with trembling hands, as yet another guard approached on a dragon. *What if...*

"Mythrién! Myth riel ish ilen!" Kieron shouted at the guard's dragon. It raised its head in confusion.

"Non aluein ish il riél!" Kieron ordered the beast to stop. "Nathran!"

It tilted its head.

Not used to hearing your own language, huh? Kieron smirked.

"Al an al uth riél." Kieron reminded the dragon that it was now free. "Uth vas riél!"

It's eyes focused on the land in the distance.

"Attack!" the guard shouted, nudging the dragon forward, but it hovered in front of Vâken and Kieron, refusing the order.

Kieron took aim at the guard atop the confused dragon. "This is your chance. Take it. Nathran! Ul ilien! Uth riél!" Kieron ordered the beast to fly away, reminding it again that it was now free to return to its home.

"Fly away!" Kieron shouted at it.

And to his surprise, the beast obeyed. It turned and flew away. The guard struggled with the reins to control the dragon, but it was no use. The dragon flew off toward its home, spinning in air until its rider leapt off.

The desire for freedom proved to be more powerful than its master's desire for victory.

Kieron realized that fact would be their key to victory, not violent bloodshed. He turned Vâken and flew to locate Théan in the fray.

Kealy caught up to him. "Where are you going?"

"Speak to the dragons! Remind them of their freedom," Kieron shouted. "Their desire to be free will cause them to fly away."

Kealy's eyes widened. "What?"

"It's true!" he shouted above the wind as Vâken flew. "I just spoke to a dragon, and it worked." Kieron heeled Vâken's ribs to make it go faster. "I have to tell the others."

"But..." Kealy's mouth turned downward. "I don't know dragonspeak."

"Yes you do!" Kieron shouted. "All elves do. Search deep within yourself, Kealy. You know the language. It's there. Try!" Kieron and Vâken flew off.

Kealy spotted a guard approaching on a wyvern dragon at high speed. Kieron turned to see her load her bow and take aim.

No, Kealy. Just try to speak the language of the dragons, he thought. *You know it. Dragonspeak is deep inside your heart. Try.*

And then he saw Kealy slowly lower her bow.

"Yes. That's it," Kieron murmured.

The approaching dragon hesitated in midair for a moment, and then flew away with its rider desperately trying to stop it.

"Yes!" Kieron shouted to Kealy. She turned and offered him a wide smile. "Keep going."

Vâken zigzagged as it searched for Kieron's brother, Théan.

"There!" he shouted to his dragon. Up ahead, Théan shot his arrow at one of Valbrand's guards, piercing his shoulder. He fell off the dragon and tumbled through the air.

"Théan," Kieron said as he approached.

"One more kill." Théan shot him a pleased grin and raised his arm in victory. "Yes!"

"Use dragonspeak to remind the dragons that they are free to return home." Kieron pointed to a dragon, flying away without its rider.

"What?"

"It will work, trust me. It will be much better than staining Vulgaard fields red with blood."

"But I don't—"

"Yes you do! You know dragonspeak. "We all do. You've just forgotten it. We have taken on the ways of men and used violence instead. Do it, Théan! Speak the language," Kieron urged. "The time for violence will come and we will fight with bow and arrows, with swords and spears. But not this day." He turned Vâken and flew away.

"Brilliant!" Théan flew off to inform the others.

Kieron and Vâken hovered over Vulgaard, watching the scene as dozens of dragons abandoned the fight and their riders, sending them tumbling to their deaths on the hard earth below.

Thyler and Aerin also used dragonspeak to free the guards' dragons. They cheered when they saw more and more dragons abandon the fight and fly off.

"Yes!" Thyler shook his fist into the air.

More and more guards fell to the ground. Some survived the fall, but fell into the hands of General Aluein's soldiers, or stood with arms raised in surrender before angry elves.

The heartwarming sight of the freed dragons flying to their homelands brought a wide grin to Kieron's face. "This is how it should be. Dragons deserve to be free." He thought of Fawn, and pictured the little dragon grazing in the fields, free to live again.

"Quite a beautiful sight, yes?" Kealy said as she and her dragon approached. "I even told Söen here to fly home if she wants to, but she told me she wants to be part of the battle for Vulgaard and Théadril."

Kieron stroked Vâken's neck, damp with sweat. "Is this true for you, boy?"

The dragon squawked and flew off to meet the others that had landed in the tall grass. The riders hopped off their dragons and led them to a small pond to drink.

Hundreds of elves celebrated the victory over Valbrand's Riders of Rünbrior and prison guards.

The Rünbrior prison was finally destroyed, once and for all.

No dragon would ever be abducted and enslaved within the Ranvieg mountains again. Valbrand would have to find some other way to have his precious gold coins.

The Dragon Games were finally over.

"So," Kieron began. "You understand dragonspeak now?" he teased Kealy, who grinned sheepishly.

"I guess you were right. I do have it deep within me." She playfully shoved Kieron.

"We all do. We have just forgotten." He twisted the bow in his hands. "We were too quick to embrace the ways of men. Prince Thætil and the queen can understand this. Their dragon riders must know how to speak to their dragons so they can ride as one."

"One day you'll be among them, Kieron." Kealy patted his shoulder. "I just know it."

∽

Kieron stood and made his way over to Vâken.

"Where are you going?" Théan asked. He put his hands on his hips.

"I'm not sure. But when I am settled, I will tell you," Kieron replied.

"What are you talking about?" Théan asked,

Kieron lowered his head. "I mean…I'm not returning home. I can't.

As Kieron spoke, many of the elves began to walk away from the pond and toward the field. One by one, they made their way over to some activity through the tall grass, craning their necks and pointing to the distance.

"What is it?" Kealy asked. She spotted a caravan of horses coming over the hill. "Kieron, I think you should see this."

The caravan of the queen's guards rode in unison over the hills. The banner of Queen Ragnalla, held by a rider in the lead, flapped in the wind.

Théan and his friends trotted over to the road's edge and bowed along with the others as the riders passed by. Kieron slowly approached. His mouth dropped open when he saw Prince Thætil atop his white stallion, riding toward him. His white leather armor stood out, as did his white braided hair and piercing blue eyes.

The queen's brother, Prince Thætil, made his way over to an astonished Kieron. The crowd parted and watched the scene. Kieron gulped, wondering what the prince wanted with him.

He bowed. "Your Highness."

"Is this Kieron Gaardœn, son of Lars Gaardœn of Glouslow?" Prince Thætil asked.

Kieron nodded.

"Speak up," one of Prince Thætil's guards ordered.

The prince raised his hand and gave his guard a stern look. He stepped toward the trembling Kieron, towering over the young elf.

"Yes, sir." Kieron murmured.

"I have heard great things about your bravery inside the prison and out here in battle atop your dragon." The prince smiled.

Kieron bowed again.

"He helped save us all by speaking to the dragons." Kealy stepped up. When the prince turned toward her, she bowed. "Your Highness."

Prince Thætil faced Kieron. "You speak dragonspeak?"

Kieron nodded. "Yes, sir."

"Well done." He raised his hand and gained the attention of the stunned crowd. His braided white hair fell across his shoulder, and the silver crown on his brow sparkled in the light of the rising moon. "Young Kieron, I have come to thank you." The prince bowed, causing many gasps from the watching crowd.

"Your Highness," Kieron said. "This is an honor."

"Because of your bravery and that of your friends," he said, motioning toward Thyler, Aerin, and Kealy, "many enslaved dragons are now free. You helped Prince Peter of Illiath free many slaves as well."

"I only did what I could do," Kieron said.

"I have been asked by the queen to invite you to her palace, where her Dragon Riders are preparing to head to Théadril and fight with King Alexander of Illiath."

"Long live the king!" shouted a man from the crowd.

Théan approached and bowed. "Your Highness," he began. "Young Kieron is expected at home. May I first return him to our parents?"

Kieron grimaced.

"They are extremely concerned about him." Théan squeezed Kieron's shoulder.

"By all means," Prince Thætil replied. "In the morning, make your way to your family, and then join the others as they fly to the palace at Vulgaard, where you will begin your training. Prince Thurdin, the queen's son, is there to train alongside you all. You and your friends, young Kieron." He offered them a warm smile, as though he understood he had just made their dreams come true.

"Yes, sir." Kieron turned and smiled at Kealy and the others, beaming with excitement.

"Together, we all will fight to save Vulgaard and Théadril from the Darkness." Prince Thætil turned to leave. The crowd erupted in cheers and yelps.

Kealy tapped Kieron's shoulder. "What an honor," she whispered as they watched the prince and his guards mount their horses and trot off toward General Aluein's encampment.

"I can't believe it!" Thyler shouted. "We're heading to the palace to train as…as royal Dragon Riders."

Aerin's face turned pale. "I can't believe it, too."

"You look like you're going to be sick. You'd better sit down." Kealy helped him to the ground.

Kieron motioned for Vâken to come to him. His dragon obeyed.

"But first, you will come with me to see Mother and Father in the morning." Théan placed his heavy hand onto Kieron's shoulder again. "Understand? I promised them."

Kieron winced. "Alright." He sighed as he stepped away from his brother's grip.

"Help me set up camp."

Kieron assisted his brother in making beds for himself, the boys, and Kealy from gathered grass. They gathered stones and made fire pits. Small fires were lit to warm them throughout the night.

As the moon rose and the stars appeared like glitter across the black sky, Kieron tried to reconstruct the day's events, but each time he did, his heart beat so fast that he could barely breathe. His legs twitched as he thought about running through the caves within the prison.

"Get some sleep," Théan ordered.

"I'm trying to." Kieron rolled over. Picturing himself atop Vâken heading into battle with Prince Peter, Prince Thætil, and Kealy brought a wide smile to his face, but made it almost impossible to sleep. *Has my day finally arrived? The day when I can at last say to others that I am officially a Dragon Rider?*

"What's the matter?" Théan asked as he packed up his saddle the next morning. He stretched his back and neck.

Kieron tossed dirt onto the fire pit and stomped on it with his feet. "Nothing."

"Your grumpy face has returned so soon after yesterday's victories?" Théan chuckled.

"You know why."

"Kieron, Mother and Father long to see that you are alive again. You won't understand their angst until you yourself are a father." Théan took his leather water pouch to the pond to fill it. "Wash up, and then we'll head home."

"Why does war have to happen?" Kieron huffed.

"What?"

"I simply wanted to win in the Dragon Games and then join the Queen's Dragon Riders to protect the land, not fight in war."

"You have Lord Bedlam to thank. He's the one who caused all this trouble." Théan bent down at the pond's edge and filled his water pouch.

"Why does he hate King Alexander so much?" Kieron asked Théan.

"Because his son, Peter, is the chosen one." He attached his water pouch to the saddle and then carried it to his waiting dragon, munching on damp grass.

"Whatever did the young prince do to Lord Bedlam?" Kieron

handed Vâken some grass to eat.

"Prince Peter had entered the Dragon Forest and lived. That's what alerted Lord Bedlam that his power over the rulers was coming to an end. He has set his sights on the Dragon Forest. To destroy the Dragon Forest is to destroy the Dragon and the protection of the people." Théan adjusted his saddle and the reins attached to his dragon's bit. "Including all of us in Vulgaard."

Kieron couldn't imagine the destruction of the Dragon Forest, let alone the giant dragon he had seen flying through the air the day before. It had blotted out the sun.

"The only kingdom that stands in Lord Bedlam's way is Illiath." Théan removed a map from his saddle bag and unfolded it. He pointed to the land to the north. "See?"

On the map, Kieron could see the crude drawing of Vulgaard and Théadril with Illiath within its boundaries. To the north was the Dragon Forest.

"So that's the Dragon Forest," Kieron mumbled to himself. "It seems so far away."

"Don't you have a saddle?" Théan asked.

Kieron shook his head. "Vâken found me as I was escaping. There was no time to locate a saddle in that horrid place."

Théan exhaled loudly, and Kieron knew his brother was frustrated. "Stay here. I'll go find one."

Kieron spotted Thyler and Kealy preparing their dragons to head off to train.

"I thought you were heading home" Thyler asked.

"Théan is finding me a saddle. And then we head home." Kieron frowned.

"You should go make peace with your family, Kieron." Thyler fed more grass to his dragon. "We all are heading to war. You never know when you'll see them again."

"What about you? Aren't you heading home first?"

Thyler lowered his eyes. "I have asked many elves over there about Heinland's Gate, the region I grew up in. They tell me it was scorched, and that my family made their way south. I will find them after the war."

Kieron pictured his own family marching through the woods, carrying all they owned. His little sisters, holding hands and crying in fear, made the anger inside him boil.

"How did all this hatred between Lord Bedlam and King Alexander begin, anyway?" Kieron picked up a rock and threw it away.

"If you really want answers, I'll show you the one who has the answers." Thyler walked Kieron to a group of elves speaking with a tall, wiry wizard dressed in a long white robe.

"Shh," Thyler instructed. "Be very quiet as he speaks. He's very wise."

Kieron leaned in and saw the old man with a long white beard speak to the elfin riders about the plan of attack.

"Who is that?" Kieron asked.

"That is Theo; he's a wise wizard tutor to Prince Peter. He's been telling us about the battle plans. He's the one to ask about why Lord Bedlam hates King Alexander." Thyler patted Kieron's shoulder and walked away.

Kieron watched as the elves listened to the wizard speak about how they will fly to the land surrounding the Dragon Forest. When he was finished, he dismissed the troops and turned to make his way to the palace.

"What do you want?" Theo asked as he walked away.

Kieron followed him. "I…I don't know. My friend said that—"

"Who?" he asked without turning around.

"My friend, Thyler. He told me to ask you my questions."

"Questions about what?"

"Well, questions about the looming war…"

The wizard shook his head.

"And about the battle…"

He kept walking.

"And about why Lord Bedlam hates King Alexander. Why do leaders of men allow the land to be harmed this way?"

The wizard stopped midstride. He slowly turned around with a perplexed look on his face.

Kieron stopped and stared with eyebrows raised. *Maybe I shouldn't have asked.*

"Mythrien il eluen alas," the wizard said.

Kieron's eyes widened. "You speak dragonspeak?"

"Aye. And so do you."

"Yes."

"So, you asked about Lord Bedlam and King Alexander."

"I figured that since I am about to fly into battle to save a kingdom and a forest I have never seen, maybe it would help to know why I am going."

The wizard squinted his eyes and studied the young elf before him. "Maybe you should know, young Kieron."

Kieron stepped back. "How do you know my name?"

CHAPTER 13

T heo grinned. "You seek answers, young elf?"

"I do." Kieron raised his chin. "I have just been through hell inside that mountain prison and almost lost a dear friend in battle with Valbrand's guards. I deserve answers."

"Do you now?" Theo stared down at the young elf before him. "And your brother? Won't he miss you?"

Kieron turned to see Théan placing a saddle onto Vâken's back and strapping it on. "If we aren't gone too long, he won't miss me."

"Let us away then." Theo ordered an elfin guard to place Kieron onto a waiting dragon. Before he knew it, he was atop a dragon, heading toward the palace of Vulgaard, which shimmered in the bright morning sun like a jewel.

As they stood at the gate entrance to the palace, Kieron gazed upward at the glimmering structure. He had only seen the beautiful castle from afar. Now, standing at the gates, Kieron thought it was something out of a dream.

"It really is made of diamonds," Kieron whispered to himself. "I thought it was a myth."

"Come with me, and I'll show you why your people are about to embark on this mission of liberty," the wizard said. His robe flowed behind him as he walked, and it seemed like he was floating, like a spirit.

"So...who are you? Why were the others listening to you?" Kieron asked.

But Theo stood silent as they waited for the guard to open the gate.

"Master Sirus," the guard said. He glanced down at Kieron with an emotionless face. When he opened the gate, Theo walked through it. Kieron hesitated.

"Aren't you coming?" the wizard asked.

Taking a deep breath, Kieron entered the palace grounds, unsure as to what lie ahead. He'd heard about wizards, and even visited one in the next town. But that wizard was good for making potions to help sick people. This wizard seemed to be more important, especially if he lived within the palace walls.

Once they approached the massive double doors, guarded by more imposing elfin males, Kieron felt his stomach flip. *I don't think I belong here.*

"Um, I've changed my mind. I should probably get back to the camp. I don't want to be gone for too long and miss out on further instructions." He started to turn to leave, but the bony hand of the wizard rested on his shoulder, sending a shiver through him.

"Come with me." Theo smiled, and his pale blue eyes sparkled almost like dragon's eyes did when thrilled. "I think you'll enjoy this."

When the doors opened, a young elfin male stood in the doorway. "Theo," the young male said. "To what do we owe this pleasure?"

"Prince Thurdin," the wizard said. "Your Highness." He turned and waved to Kieron. "I have brought this young elf from Glouslow to learn more about the origin of the Darkness before he rides into battle."

Thurdin tilted his head back. "Ah. Yes. A history lesson from Theo." He moved aside so they could walk into the grand entrance of the palace. "Far be it from me to interrupt one of your lessons."

"Thurdin, here, is also a very skilled dragon rider." Theo made his way to the center of the space.

"Hello, Your Highness," Kieron said in a soft voice, revealing his nervousness. "I'm Kieron."

"Nothing to be nervous about." Thurdin motioned for him to follow him. "This is the people's palace. All elves are welcome to come here and learn more about the queen, the palace, and all of Vulgaard."

"Really?" Kieron glanced all around. "I never knew that. I always thought it was forbidden." The room glistened like ice. He carefully approached the walls and saw his reflection in them. Even the floor looked like ice; it shone and sparkled. The large picture windows framed the rolling green hills and valleys below. Above him was the painted ceiling of a mural, depicting the history of Vulgaard. The crystal chandelier hung low, capturing the sunlight streaming in from the windows, sending its hundreds of tiny prisms of light bouncing off every surface in the room.

"Well, do you have any questions for me, Kieron?" Thurdin rocked back and forth on his heels.

Kieron, still wide-eyed from the splendor of the room, shook his head.

"Are you sure? Well, I admire that you want to learn more about the reasons for the war before heading into battle. It shows you have great desire to learn." Thurdin smiled at Theo. "I'll leave you two alone, then. Enjoy." Thurdin made his way up the stairs to his room.

"Come this way." Theo motioned for Kieron to follow him down a long corridor lined with windows on one side and framed paintings of kings and queens of Vulgaard.

"Where are we going?" Kieron asked as he walked and glanced out the windows to the gates below, where he had stood just a few minutes before.

"We are going to a place that will answer your many questions. Since you are an elf of Vulgaard, you deserve to know the history of the land that you are connected to."

They turned the corner and entered the largest room Kieron had ever seen. The palace library reached thirty to forty feet high and was made up of bookshelves from floor to ceiling, filled with so many books, Kieron felt dizzy as he glanced around. "I didn't know this many books existed in the world."

Theo chuckled. "And this is only one of the palace libraries." He made his way over to a set of books and removed one of them. "I think we shall look at this book first." He carried it over to a marble-top table with ornate, gilded legs. He pulled out a chair for Kieron to sit on and then opened the book for them to read through together.

"Is it true you know Prince Peter?" Kieron asked.

"Know him? Ha!" Theo said as he removed his pipe from a pocket inside his robe. "I'm his tutor."

Kieron remained near the door, still glancing around the room with his mouth agape.

"I also tutored his father, the king.Sit here, boy," Theo ordered. He tapped his finger on an open page in the book. "We shall begin here."

Kieron obeyed Theo's orders and approached the book resting on the table. He leaned over it and saw the title of the chapter: "The Darkness."

"Whoa," he murmured under his breath. "Who wrote this book?"

"I helped the late Queen Ragnalla chronicle what had occurred in Vulgaard years ago, to help future generations, such as yourself, understand what had happened and why."

Kieron sat on the large, comfy chair and scooted it close to the table. "So you're a teacher and a wizard. The wizard in our town is a healer; nothing more."

"Hmm. Nothing more?" Theo squinted with one eye at his new pupil. "Each wizard has its purpose." He tapped his long finger on the cover of the book. "Well, then. Let's begin."

Kieron felt a chill run over his body.

"Long ago," Theo began. "When peace reigned in Vulgaard, a prophecy was told to the king. In this prophecy, the wizard to the king warned him that a time of darkness would come." Theo leaned in. "And this concerned the king and the men of his kingdom." He raised his finger into the air. "But, the wizard also said there was hope. A dragon would come to bring together all the lands as one and restore the peace." He turned a page that revealed a sketch of the Dragon.

"The Great Dragon of the Forest?" Kieron asked. He studied the sketch of the beast in flight.

Theo made his way around the table. "Yes. As you know, elves can speak the language of the dragons. They formed a bond millennia ago. The elves have worked hard to keep that bond firmly in place, communicating with dragons about their needs. But with man? This is not the case. Long ago, men abused the dragons and hurt them, stole their precious gemstones, and destroyed any chance of forming a bond."

"They abuse them still." Kieron frowned as he remembered what he had seen in the prison; Fawn's shivering body, scarred from weeks of abuse. "They remove the fire glands from the dragons so they cannot defend themselves."

Theo grimaced and rubbed his throat, as though he felt the dragon's pain. "Things were far worse back then."

How could things be much worse? Kieron thought.

"But Elfin women bred with men, and some of these children were gifted with special abilities. Some could also communicate with dragons." Theo turned the page. A drawing of a lovely young girl with gentle features and flowing dark tresses was on one page. Kieron thought her beautiful. The name Laurien was written underneath her picture.

"One young girl lived here in this palace, where she learned about her gifts and about dragons. She cared for them and gained their trust. Unfortunately, due to her kindness and love of dragons, she was bewitched by the one evil dragon that could cause more harm than any good."

Kieron listened intently.

"As a result, the dragon persuaded her to ask the queen's wizard to cast a spell. A unique spell that had only been cast one other time."

"What was that spell?"

"To turn a dragon into a man."

Kieron's brows rose.

"The queen allowed it. And so, the dragon was turned into a man with a spell cast by the king's wizard. That man…" Theo hesitated.

"Was Lord Bedlam?" Kieron said.

Theo nodded. "Yes. And the wizard that cast the spell…"

Kieron pushed the chair back and stood. "You?"

"Yes." Theo placed his hands onto the book.

"But how? Why? How can such a spell exist? I've never heard of such a thing." Kieron thought about the stories his grandmother used to tell him.

"I know of such a spell and I used it, against my better judgment. But I only did it because it was foretold." Theo slid the book over to Kieron to read.

"No." Kieron shook his head. "That's impossible."

"Read the book."

Kieron pushed it away. "You are the one responsible for bestowing upon my people…and the lands…this evil presence called Lord Bedlam, and now you want me to read this book and gloss over your role in all this? Do you know how many lives have been damaged or lost because of the Darkness? How many dragons have suffered? The land won't produce crops like it used to. The winters last longer, making the ground hard. And all this was because of a spell cast on a dragon to transform him into a man?"

"You asked the question about the origin of the Darkness, and I have told you." Theo started to leave the room

"Wait," Kieron said to Theo's back. "I don't understand. How can you just walk away from this?"

But Theo did walk away and headed toward the library entrance.

"And how can Queen Thordis just ignore your role in all this…this disaster?" Kieron raced after him.

As Theo left the room, Kieron gave up following him and returned to the book, still lying open on the table. He stared at it for a moment and then began to read the words about the Dragon of Promise.

"After the Dragon of Promise returned to the forest, the swords were forged by Laurien, the promised queen of Illiath, betrothed to King Alexander," he read. "In the swords, a special code was inscribed. A code no one would know, especially Lord Bedlam. He had commissioned the swords to give to the ten rulers of men as a gift to gain their trust." Kieron ran his finger over the drawing of the swords, glanced up, and thought about it. He knew of the swords, and how some had been lost. King Alexander had sent his knights on a quest to find each sword. He continued reading.

"Once all the ten swords are gathered together, only then can the code be deciphered and the truth revealed. Until then, the Darkness will remain." The chapter ended, so Kieron turned the page, but nothing more was written. He slammed the book shut and turned to leave.

"Excuse me," Prince Thurdin said, startling Kieron.

"What?" Kieron clutched his chest. "You scared me. I didn't see you standing there."

Thurdin grinned slightly and reached for the book. Kieron stepped out of his way.

"We don't appreciate our books being treated so poorly." Thurdin picked up the book.

"Sorry," Kieron said. He studied the prince's eyes and noticed they were different than when they had first met in the foyer. "Are…are you alright?"

"Yes, why?" Thurdin made his way to the bookshelf.

"Your eyes, they look…different."

Thurdin returned the book to its proper place next to previous chronicles of Vulgaardian history. "I'm fine."

Kieron shrugged and started to leave to find Theo.

"Well, actually I am not fine," Prince Thurdin said. He turned to face Kieron.

"Pardon me, Your Highness." Kieron stopped.

"You see, we royals take it personally when locals come into the palace and mistreat our tomes." He waved his hand. "These are priceless and precious books, irreplaceable records of our history."

"I understand. I'm sorry it seemed like I was abusing the book. I wasn't. I was just a little upset at something I was told." Kieron turned to leave again.

"About Lord Bedlam?" Prince Thurdin asked.

Kieron exhaled and turned toward the prince again. "Yes. Well, mostly about what Theo had done."

Thurdin slowly made his way over to Kieron, his eyes intensely focused on him. Kieron took a step back. "What Theo did upsets you?"

"Yes."

"Because the act of turning a dragon into a man goes against the natural order of things?"

Kieron thought about it. "Yes, I suppose so."

Thurdin came closer to Kieron. "But I thought you understood dragons. Can you not speak their languages?"

"Yes, of course I can. All elves can."

"Do you not think a dragon out there just might want to become a man?" Thurdin glanced out the window.

"No," Kieron replied without hesitation.

"Really?"

"Really. In fact, there's no reason a dragon would want to become a man unless it was forced to, or wanted to just to harm men," Kieron said.

He could see in Thurdin's eyes that he was considering what Kieron had said. But after a few seconds, he replied, "Interesting that you would think this way."

"Why? I know dragons. They are happy creatures as they are. They love to fly and live their lives in the mountains or forests. Being human would take all that away. They'd have to rely on others for everything. That goes against their nature."

Thurdin tossed his head back and laughed. "You know nothing of what you speak."

Kieron furrowed his brow. Thurdin's voice sounded strange.

"Lord Bedlam relies on no one. He lives his life the way he wants to. If he wants to fly, he can. If he wants to ride a horse, he can. No one and nothing can nor will ever stop him, especially any one dragon."

"You…" Kieron carefully studied the changed prince before him. "You speak of Bedlam as if you know and admire him."

"*Lord* Bedlam," he corrected Kieron. "And, yes, I do admire him."

"But why? After all the pain he has caused this land and the people." Kieron stepped closer to the library entryway. "And the dragons."

"He hasn't cause any pain. All he has done is fulfill his destiny." Thurdin stepped toward Kieron.

"No, he hasn't. He has cast a spell on the land. This Darkness is his doing. My father has to till the ground for many months now to plant. Life is harder for elves. I have heard how Lord Bedlam cast a spell on the Duke of Illiath, and how he tried to kill King Alexander. Lord Bedlam allowed Prince Peter to be imprisoned against his will. He's after the land and won't rest until he—"

"Enough!" Prince Thurdin shoved Kieron into the wall.

As the pain and panic rose within him, Kieron ran out of the library and raced down the hall, desperately searching for anyone to help him. But no one was around. "Theo!" he shouted.

He turned and ran down another hallway until he encountered a few elfin guards. "Help," he said, trying to catch his breath.

"What is it?" the guard asked.

"Thurdin," Kieron started. "The prince…"

The guard looked behind Kieron, searching the hallway for the prince.

"He's gone mad. Something's happened to him. He's talking like a crazy person." Kieron pointed behind him. "He's back there in the library."

The guards looked at each other and then trotted off toward the library.

Kieron bent over, trying to catch his breath.

"You don't know who you are messing with," a voice said from a darkened hallway.

Kieron looked up and saw the prince walking toward him. His eyes glowed red.

"You think you know, but you have no idea." Prince Thurdin approached him.

Kieron turned to run, but the prince stopped him. "If you tell anyone about what you have seen here…" he threatened.

"What?" Kieron asked,

"I will make sure your family is gone forever."

"No!" Kieron started to run off, but ran into Theo instead.

"Theo!" Prince Thurdin said. "Are we glad to see you."

"What's going on here? This boy looks frightened."

"I don't know. I turned the corner and found him. I believe he is lost." Thurdin placed his hand on Kieron's shoulder and squeezed. "I know this palace is so vast and these hallways can be confusing. I apologize that we left you alone to navigate through these halls."

Kieron stared at him. Thurdin's eyes no longer glowed red, but had returned to a gray blue hue. "I'm alright," Kieron said. "Thanks."

"Come," Theo said. "I will show you the way out."

"Thank you, Theo. I would love to help our guest, but I am late for training with the others." Prince Thurdin started to head down the hallway that led to glass doors overlooking a grass lawn, where some young people stood with harnessed dragons. Kieron squinted to get a better look.

"I am helping to train Prince Peter and his friends. They are learning how to fly dragons into battle. Please excuse me." Prince Thurdin bowed, never taking his eyes of Kieron.

"No," Kieron said. He took hold of Theo's arm.

"What is it?" Theo asked.

"Yes, what is it?" Thurdin asked. One eyebrow rose as he waited for Kieron to reply, reminding him of the threat.

Kieron thought about the dilemma. "It's just that…"

"Yes?" Theo asked.

"I was wondering if I could see the training session. You see, I have much experience with dragon riding. I'd love to watch."

Thurdin narrowed his eyes and shot him a venomous look.

"Well, I'm not sure if there's time. We leave for Illiath in the morning. All the troops are getting into place," Theo explained. "Perhaps some other time."

"Yes, perhaps some other time." Thurdin smiled. "I am intrigued. I must say, I'd love to observe your riding skills. But I am sure we will fly together in battle, where you can show me your prowess."

Kieron stood close to Theo. "Yes. Perhaps."

"Come, let me walk you back to the camps, and I'll answer any further questions you may have for me." Theo motioned for Kieron to head toward the foyer.

Prince Thurdin smiled and turned to head to the grass lawn where Prince Peter and his friends stood.

CHAPTER 14

Once outside, Kieron grabbed hold of Theo's arm. "You have   to listen to me."

But the guards appeared to open the gates for them, so Kieron held his tongue until they had made their way through the gates and down the path.

"What is it?' Theo asked.

"Listen…" Kieron glanced around for crows in the trees. "You need to hear this."

"Why are you whispering?" Theo asked.

"Because there are spies everywhere." Kieron saw the troops ahead. "And I don't want anyone else to hear this."

"Go on." Theo stopped and looked at the elfin boy with a quizzical brow.

"Back there, in the library. Prince Thurdin…there's something wrong with him."

Theo tilted his head. "Wrong with him?"

Kieron nodded. "Yes. His eyes…there was something wrong with them. And his voice, it had changed. He threatened me."

Theo looked back at the palace.

"And he said he admired Lord Bedlam."

Theo grabbed Kieron's arm and dragged him into the woods so no one could see them. "What did you say, boy?"

Kieron grimaced from the tight grip. He sensed the urgency.

Theo released his arm. "Tell me everything he said."

"It seemed Prince Thurdin admired Bedlam. He became incensed when I didn't include the title *Lord* Bedlam. He corrected me. It was as if he admired the evil lord."

Theo stared off to the distance with a disquieted look on his face.

"And he went on and on about how powerful Bedlam is, and how he doesn't rely on anyone. It was strange."

"His eyes," Theo said. "You mentioned his eyes. What about them?"

Kieron thought about it. "They glowed red for a moment."

Upon hearing those words, Theo stepped back as though hit in the chest by an arrow.

"What is it? What do you think is wrong with him? He was so kind at first, and then…Theo, he threatened my family. Are they safe? Was I wrong to tell you?" Kieron's eyes welled with tears.

Theo grabbed his shoulders. "You were right to tell me. Tomorrow we fly into battle. I will have to warn Prince Thætil about what happened. Your family, I will ensure they are brought to the palace where they will be safe. I promise."

"Thank you." Kieron sighed with relief. "Theo, what happened to Prince Thurdin? I know you know. Tell me."

Theo paced for a moment in deep thought, and Kieron sensed the wizard was thinking about possibilities. "The other day, while training in the Maze, we sensed the presence of Lord Bedlam trying to tempt Prince Peter and his friends toward his evil power. But his presence never materialized. It was all part of the test." Theo turned to Kieron. "But it seems he did tempt one."

"Prince Thurdin?"

Theo didn't answer. His eyes showed his concern. His brow furrowed, and the corners of his mouth downturned.

"Theo…who are you, really?" Something inside Kieron tugged at him to asked that question. The mysterious man or wizard before him seemed to have layers known only by a few.

Theo turned to the young elf before him and looked down his long thin nose at him, hesitant to answer.

"I know, it's none of my business," Kieron said defeatedly. He turned to head over to the camp to find Kealy and tell her about what he had encountered in the palace.

"Kieron," Theo said. "Your name means one who walks in darkness."

The boy stopped and turned around. "My mother named me that

because I was born at night, in the dark."

Theo smiled. "But you have a light within you. You are not in darkness at all. In fact, you despise the Darkness Lord Bedlam has caused this land, because you are drawn to the light with such fierceness that you cannot explain it, can you?"

Kieron shook his head.

"I am the wizard appointed to the kings and queens of Vulgaard long ago. I serve at the pleasure of Queen Thordis." He bowed.

"I see." Kieron narrowed his eyes. "But I sense there is more to you than you are telling me. For instance, how can you know what I am drawn to, and everything like that?"

Theo grinned and tapped his temple with his long bony finger. "A wizard's mind knows much."

"Oh?" Kieron made his way over to him. "I have a feeling you know more about Lord Bedlam than you are letting on."

"This is true. It is wise, always wise, to know who your enemy is so you can do your best to anticipate his every move." Theo stared at the palace and the mountains. "I do know him and where he came from."

"He was once a dragon. How did you transform him? Does he still have the powers of a dragon? If so, that's quite a formidable foe."

"Yes. He is." A faraway look came to Theo's eyes. "I had to transform him. It went against everything inside me, but I had to do it. It had been foretold for a very important reason."

"And now he is our enemy, more powerful than any—"

"No." Theo jerked his head around to face Kieron. "Not more powerful than the Dragon of the Forest."

Kieron saw that the sparkle had returned to Theo's eyes. Hope had returned to his eyes. "You're right." He pointed to the sky. "I saw it fly through the air and transform into a white owl. It was magnificent."

"My boy." Theo patted his shoulder. "That is only the beginning. You are about to see many more magnificent things on this journey. You will grow much from it."

Kieron smiled.

"Now it is time for you to go back to the camp and hear your instructions for the battle."

"But Prince Thurdin and the spell he's under. What about—"

"That is for me to handle. And I will handle it. Now go on. I will inform the elfin guards to bring your parents to the palace once the prince and the others head out to battle. They will be safe there, I promise."

"But Lord Bedlam was able to get to him. What if he is able to get to my parents?"

"Trust me, he will soon be so busy with the battle that the palace happenings will be the least of his concerns."

"The swords," Kieron mumbled.

"Yes. His priority is getting to the Dragon Forest with all the swords."

"Will he?" Kieron cocked his head. "Will he win, Theo?"

"He is powerful, this is true. But he remains incapable of being in two places at once. His minions will be forced to be with him in the battle as well. The palace will soon be the safest place for your parents."

Theo walked with Kieron out of the woods. "One thing Lord Bedlam doesn't have that Prince Peter does."

"What's that?"

"Love." Theo smiled. "He may have his minions, but he doesn't have all the friends and community that Prince Peter has. All of you have answered the call to go and defend what is right, what is true." Theo winked. "Now that's love."

Kieron smiled.

They glanced around for any crows, circling above.

"So, do you have all the answers to your questions?" Theo said after a while.

Kieron furrowed his brow. "Yes."

"Sometimes it is best to not have all the answers, hmm?"

The corner of Kieron's mouth curled and his stomach ached. "You're right." He remembered the joy of flying his dragon over the hills of Glouslow with the summer sun on his back. The only cares he had were his chores. *I miss those days.*

"We all miss those days." Theo grinned.

Kieron's eyes widened. "What? Wait, how did you know I was thinking that just—"

"Get back to your brother. Say goodbye to your family. And prepare for battle. Good luck to you. Be safe. Fly well."

Kieron ran out of the woods toward the camp. "I will. Always!"

he shouted.

∽

Kieron leapt over tall grass, running as fast as he could to where his brother stood, huffing angrily.

"Where have you been?" Théan shouted at him.

"At the palace of Vulgaard!" Kieron bent over, trying to catch his breath.

"What?" Théan glared at him. "What are you talking about? The palace is miles away." He pointed to the glimmering structure in the distance.

Kieron nodded. "I know. And I was there. I flew on a dragon with the wizard Theo. I saw the palace library, met Prince Thurdin, …all of it."

"I think you have gone insane, little brother. Now get onto that dragon and follow me before I take this stick and tan your hide but good!" Théan shook a twig from a tree branch.

"It's true," Thyler said as he approached. "He flew off with the wizard Theo. I saw it."

Théan's face crinkled. "Whatever for?"

"I asked him my questions, and he answered them by showing me a book…a history book. Théan, I know the secret of Lord Bedlam and why we are waging war against him."

Théan straightened and a serious look befell his face. "Kieron," he began. "What have you done?"

"All I did was get the answers to my questions."

Théan searched the skies.

"Crows?" Kieron asked.

"Come. We must get you home to see Mother and Father before you are discovered." Théan took Kieron's arm and led him to Vâken.

"Good luck!" Thyler shouted as the two brothers took off. "I'll see you when you get back."

∽

Away from the Ranvieg Mountains, no one would ever know a

war loomed. The forest was peaceful, the birds sang, and the autumn air blew cold and crisp through Kieron's hair. He could almost forget the events of the last few days.

Almost.

Deep in his heart, he didn't want to go home. He wanted to see his mother again, but he didn't want to face his father's wrath and gaze into his disappointed eyes again.

Kieron sighed.

But it was inevitable. He had to see his family before he flew off to battle as one of the queen's Dragon Riders. He'd finally earned a chance to prove himself.

"There's the farm." Théan pointed to the land below.

Scarred by the fire, it looked like a victim of an attack. Not much was left of the house Kieron had been born in. He glanced to the west and saw the caves that were once the dragon stalls. His heart sank even deeper, knowing the dragons would never be with him again.

Théan landed his dragon in the patch of grass near the woods behind the house. Kieron did the same. He hopped of Vâken and patted his head.

"Stay here, boy. I won't be long, and then we can head back to where the others are." Kieron felt as though his friends were now his family.

"Mother, Father?" Théan shouted into the trees.

Kieron stood with his arms crossed. He fidgeted and uncrossed his arms, then recrossed them.

Théan headed into the trees. "Mother? Father?"

Kieron took a few steps closer to the woods, wondering where his parents were.

"Hello?" he heard Théan shout from within the woods.

Silence.

Kieron's heart beat faster. *Where are they? Has something happened to them? Oh no.* He sprinted into the trees. "Mother? Father?" he shouted.

He slid to a stop when he smelled the smoke of fire and morning coffee. He spotted the firelight from the pit and his parents standing by it, warming their hands.

"Kieron!" his mother shouted, with wide eyes and arms open to greet him.

"Son!" his father cried and ran toward him.

Kieron paused then took a step back. "Father?"

"Son." His father embraced him and fell to his knees before him. "Oh son," he wept. "You're alive."

Kieron remained still for a moment, not sure what to do or feel.

"We thought the worst. But here you are. You're home again." His father parted from him and looked at him with red-rimmed eyes, tired from worry. "Son."

"Father...you're not," Kieron began. "You're not angry?"

His father shook his head. "No, my boy." He embraced Kieron even tighter. "I thought you were dead."

Kieron looked up at his mother and brother, holding each other.

"When I saw the Riders drag you away, I thought I'd lost you forever, son." His father ran his hands through Kieron's hair. "I'm so sorry, Kieron. I've been so unfair to you. I'm so sorry. I was angry, and I took it all out on you. I never should have. Can you ever forgive me, son?"

Upon hearing those words, Kieron wept and hugged his father's neck. "I'm sorry, Father. I never should have gone flying that day. I never should have let Aislinn climb onto that tree."

"No, don't blame yourself, Kieron." His father stood and put his large hands on Kieron's shoulders. "Your sister was a good sister. She just wanted to save you. That's what older brothers and sisters do. But I...I should have been the one to save you both, and I wasn't there for you or Aislinn."

Kieron hugged his father's waist. "No, Father. Don't blame yourself. Aislinn and I were foolish. We should have been home, doing our chores."

"You're a good son. And we're so glad you're home." Father and son stood, crying for a moment before Vâken squawked and interrupted them.

"Well, I see you still have your little dragon," Kieron's father said, wiping his eyes. He removed his handkerchief from his pocket and blew his nose.

"Yes, he saved my life." Kieron ran over to Vâken. "He's the fastest dragon ever."

His father gently patted Vâken's head. "There's a good boy."

Kieron looked at Vâken, and then back at his mother and brother.

After a hearty meal at the modest shelter their father had built in the woods, the family sat by the fire in the afternoon sun.

Kieron's sister, Everleigh, handed him more bread. "I baked it myself." Her white hair was pulled back into a bun, revealing her crystal blue eyes.

"It's delicious." Kieron hugged her shoulders. "It's good to be home. I didn't think I would ever see any of you again."

"It's good to have you home." His mother smiled.

"Father, I spoke with Theo, the queen's wizard." Kieron set down his cup.

"What?" His father turned to Thèan.

"That's what he told me, too."

"Father, Theo told me that Lord Bedlam has his spies everywhere. He said you all can go to the palace where you will be safe." Kieron nodded toward his siblings.

"The palace?" Everleigh sat up. "Really?"

"Kieron, we can't go to the palace." His mother shook her head. "It is many miles away. The girls cannot possibly—"

"Theo said the palace guards will come get you all tomorrow before the war begins."

"Oh mother! Can you imagine? All of us in the palace!" Everleigh hugged her little sister, Evelyn, who giggled.

"Now, hold on here…" His father set aside his meal. "We're not going anywhere."

"Father, please." Kieron's raised brows and shiny eyes told his father all he needed to know. "Please."

"Oh alright."

"Yay!" The girls shouted and clapped their hands.

"They'll come get you in the morning." Kieron grinned. "Wait 'til you see the palace." He leaned in close to his sisters. "It shines like diamonds."

"Diamonds?" Everleigh's eyes widened. "Like the queen's crown?"

He nodded.

"Is it true, Kieron?" Everleigh asked.

"What?"

"That one day you are going to be a Dragon Rider?" Her eyes sparkled.

"I sure hope so." The very thought of heading off to the palace at Vulgaard to train as an official Dragon Rider caused goosebumps on his arms.

"That's what you've always wanted!" Everleigh clapped her hands again. "I hope to join you one day."

"What an adventure you've had, huh?" their father said after hearing Kieron's stories of the Dragon Games, the escape, and his time in the palace.

"A Dragon Master?" his mother said. "I never knew there was such a thing."

"Dangler taught me so much about dragons. He showed me his book, the Dragon Chronicles, where all the wisdom of previous Dragon Masters is kept. I learned about the dragons near us and how they live." Kieron's eyes lit up. "I want to be a Dragon Master someday."

"You can be anything you want to be, Kieron." His father patted his back.

Kieron smiled, but then his heart filled with regret. It must have shown on his face, because his mother squinted at him.

"What is it, son?" she asked as she handed him a bowl of fruit.

He shook his head. "Nothing."

"Go on." She nudged him.

"Well…" Kieron didn't know how to tell them what had really happened to him inside the mountain prison, in the sky above Vulgaard, and inside the palace with Theo. But he knew he had to tell them the truth. "I rode in the battle against the prison guards."

"Yes, your brother told us about how brave you were." She smiled.

"And, well, as a result of my bravery…" He swallowed the knot in his throat. "Prince Thætil took notice of me."

"The Prince of Vulgaard? The queen's brother himself?" his father asked.

Kieron nodded. "Yes. And, well…he wants me to ride with them into battle against the Darkness."

His father's face went pale.

"Against Lord Bedlam." Kieron's eyes met his father's. The sorrow in his eyes revealed what Kieron had suspected. His father understood about the evil Lord and what going to war against him meant.

"I thought he just wanted you to come to the palace and meet the queen." His mother turned to her husband. "Is this not true?"

"Yes, well, that is true, Mother. But he also wants me to train. As a Dragon Rider. For the queen."

Everleigh's eyes widened as she listened and chewed on a biscuit. "You will be a Dragon Rider!" She squealed.

"Oh well, you can't be doing that, Kieron. You're just a boy," his mother said. She nervously adjusted her apron and started to stand, but her husband took hold of her hand to stop her.

"Now, Millie. Kieron isn't a boy anymore," his father said. "He's proven himself a man."

His mother sat back down on the log defeatedly.

"That's what the prince was saying to him, you know. When he asked him to train." Kieron's father's voice cracked with emotion.

A slight grin came to Kieron's face as he realized his father understood the situation.

"And a man has to make the decisions for his own life."

Kieron looked over at his older brother, who gave him an approving nod.

"But Lars, he's so young." His mother used her apron to dab her eyes.

"Aye. This is true. But he's seen more action today than most elfin men do their whole lives. He's ready, aren't you, son?" His father, eyes shiny with tears, nodded toward him.

"I am, Father. I am."

"Alright, then." His father stood, sniffed back the tears, and stretched his back.

"But, Father, if you need me to help around here first, I can do that. I can help you plow the field again before the frost, and I can help you hunt deer and gather wood for winter." Kieron followed his parents into the shelter.

His father turned to face him. "No, son. This is my land and my doing. This is the life I chose." With his large hands, he turned his son around to face the bright blue sky. "Out there is the life for you. You have to go out and get it. Grab hold of it with both hands and never let it go."

Kieron stared at the sky that seemed to go on forever.

"And if you happen to find someone to share it with, like I did," his father said, "then that just makes it all the better."

Kieron turned and hugged his father tightly. "I love you,

Father."

"Now go, son. You and your brother have a duty to fulfill. You go out there and fight hard for what you believe in. Fight for Vulgaard, its dragons, and all of its people." He hugged Kieron and walked away.

"We will, Father. And we'll be back soon. I promise."

Théan tapped Kieron's shoulder and walked him to their waiting dragons.

"Can I go?" Everleigh ran after them, but her mother stopped her.

"Your place is here with us, miss." She and Everleigh waved goodbye. "Don't you want to see the palace tomorrow?"

Kieron waved back. His heart pounded so fast against his chest, he could barely breathe. For the first time in his life, Kieron realized what he was about to do. Leaving his childhood and boyhood behind brought fear to his mind. The idea of saying goodbye to that part of himself forever brought tears of sorrow yet joy to his eyes.

"Goodbye!" he cried to his parents and siblings, waving to him as they stood at the opening of the shelter.

"Goodbye, son. Fly well," his father said. "Make us proud."

"I will, Father!" Kieron shouted. "Always!"

"Kieron Arrives"

CHAPTER 15

T he afternoon sun illuminated the fields below. As Kieron and Théan flew atop their dragons, Kieron watched their shadows flow over the land he had known all his life. They approached the camp site where Thyler and Aerin were placing saddles upon the backs of their dragons.

"Hello!" came a shout from behind them.

Kieron landed his dragon onto the dewy grass and hopped off to meet his friends.

"You're back." Thyler stretched out his hand.

Kieron shook it and smiled. "I am. And with my father's blessings."

Thyler's eyebrows rose. "Really?"

Kieron nodded "Yes. I am ready for what lies ahead. Tell me, what's the plan? Have you heard anything?"

Aerin pointed to the gathering of elves and men around the pond, where many were bathing or tending to wounds.

"After the battle against Valbrand's men last night, they camped here, singing songs of old and sipping that drink my grandfather sips from time to time. Makes him tipsy." Aerin stumbled back, pretending to be drunk.

"Glad you're back," Kealy shouted as her dragon landed.

"What's this?" Kieron ran to her and took hold of her dragon's reins. He patted the beast's snout.

"A new bridle for Söen." She beamed proudly.

The dragon simply munched on some cool grass.

The two watched their dragons step over to the pond to drink. Söen began splashing water onto her back. Vâken squawked and moved to the side.

"He doesn't like the water." Kieron smirked.

Kealy saw Söen step into the pond to bathe. "Hey, wait a minute, you silly dragon. Let me remove the saddle and my gear first."

Kieron made his way toward her and helped unhook the saddle.

"I love this dragon with all my heart, but if this saddle is ruined, my father will never make me another."

"You know, Kealy, you were right." Kieron carried the saddle to the pond's edge.

"I was? Well, that's a first. I seem to remember you telling me that I am never right." She chuckled as she bit into an apple.

Kieron laid the saddle onto the sandy bank of the pond. "No, I'm serious. You were right."

"About what?" She tossed him an apple.

Kieron studied the apple in his hand as he thought about his parents. "About my father."

Kealy lowered the apple. "Oh."

"I saw him last night."

Her eyes lit up. "And?"

Kieron smiled. "And you were right. He wasn't angry with me. He was angry with himself."

"Oh, Kieron." Kealy hugged his shoulders.

"He blames himself for Aislinn's death. I told him not to, because it was an accident. He apologized to me, Kealy," Kieron said with shiny eyes.

"That's wonderful, Kieron."

He bit into the apple and spittle fell onto his chin.

"And that's why you've come? I suppose you have his blessing now?" She smiled at him and used her sleeve to wipe his chin.

Kieron nodded and chomped on the apple.

"Good. Come see the others. It's an amazing sight. Elves and men, gathered together in harmony, intent on one purpose, to defeat the Darkness once and for all." She showed Kieron the campsite where hundreds of fighters gathered.

"What are they all waiting for?" he asked as he studied all the fighters congregating together.

"For the arrival of the king." She turned to her friend.

He tilted his head as though confused.

"King Alexander! He is alive and making his way here to reunite with Prince Peter." She jumped up and down. "We received word last night."

"King Alexander is alive? He's coming here to Vulgaard?" Kieron's eyes widened.

"And you'll be here to see it. You and I will ride alongside the queen's Dragon Riders, Kieron. Our dreams are about to come true." She took hold of his shoulders and playfully shook him. "Can you believe it?"

He shook his head. "It still feels like a dream."

∽

The battle to save Vulgaard and Théadril loomed. The stage was set, and the players were about to take their places on the stage. After weeks of training, Prince Peter and his friends were dragon riders themselves, and now Kieron would join them in the fight.

For days, he and Kealy helped survey the land with Prince Thætil and the other Elves. They saw with their own eyes how devastated the lands had become when King Alexander was gone, thought dead from the sorrow and despair of losing his son.

As they flew over Illiath, they saw the ruins of the king's castle. Kieron had never seen such destruction, but the Duke of Illiath, put in place by Lord Bedlam, had destroyed King Alexander's castle. The evil Duke of Illiath was bent on ending Alexander's rule once and for all.

Kealy and Kieron were there when Prince Thætil had explained to them and all his Dragon Riders about the risks of the battle.

"We are with you," Kealy said. She nudged Kieron, who nodded in agreement.

Vâken champed at the bit in its mouth.

"I know, I know. I wish you didn't have to wear that silly thing on your head and have that bit in your mouth. But it helps us communicate, and in this fight, we will need to fly as one now more than ever before. Alright?" Kieron stroked Vâken's neck.

"He's as anxious to get going as I am," Kealy said as she walked Söen over to where Kieron was. "The sooner we get going, the better. The butterflies in my belly are driving me crazy." She rubbed her belly.

"Kealy," Kieron began, "There's something I have to tell you."

"What is it?" She placed the bridle over her dragon's snout and adjusted it.

But Kieron decided the news about Lord Bedlam having cast a spell on Prince Thurdin might cause her to be afraid. "Nothing serious. I just wanted you to know that I went inside the palace and saw the library there."

Her eyes widened. "I know! That must have been a thrill."

He nodded. "It was amazing."

"What did you do in there?"

"I learned more about our mission and how important it is to Vulgaard." He took the reins into his hand.

"I agree. We mustn't fail, Kieron. If we do, the Darkness will spread and take over. The land will continue to suffer." Sorrow filled her eyes.

"We won't fail." Kieron smiled at her. "Come. Let's go join the others."

Together, they flew their dragons to the field where the other riders awaited their orders from Prince Thætil. Hundreds of elves and their dragons gathered. The sight encouraged Kieron. He knew they understood the importance of the battle against Bedlam's power and influence over several of the rulers.

The riders steadied their dragons as Prince Thætil strode to the center of the gathering. He raised his hands to silence everyone.

"Friends," Prince Thætil announced. "We are about to embark on perhaps the most important fight of our lives. As our forefathers had won many battles before, we, too must step up and defend our land, our very way of life." His long white hair, animated by the breeze, framed his strong face. "For too long, we have allowed the evil Lord Bedlam to betray our trust. For too long, we have allowed the covenant promises made between the rulers and dragons to be broken. And for too long, we have allowed the Darkness to overtake Vulgaard and Théadril. It is our time. We must now take the helm and defeat this evil presence once and for all!"

Kieron and all the riders cheered Prince Thætil. Their dragons roared and flapped their wings.

"To fail would mean the end of everything our forefathers fought for. To fail would mean an end of all that we hold dear."

He looked upon the dragons and approached one, gently stroking its head and whispering dragonspeak into its ears.

"To fail this mission would mean an end of our brotherhood with the dragons that we love and admire so much," Thætil said.

Kieron stroked Vâken's neck. "You are my brother."

"To Battle!"

The dragon nuzzled him.

"Our fathers and grandfathers taught us how to appreciate and work with the dragons in and around Vulgaard," Prince Thætil continued. "As elves, we have been given a remarkable ability to speak their language and learn their ways. Now we are about to fight to the death to preserve that bond, this brotherhood we hold dear."

More cheers rose from the crowd. Kieron's eyes welled with tears as he remembered Aislinn atop Pegasus, her beloved dragon, and how much Vâken had done for him since his time in the prison. He hugged his neck and Vâken made playful chirping sounds.

"Mount up!" Prince Thætil ordered. "Together, we will ride and fight to defeat evil once and for all." He mounted his magnificent dragon, a Draco with sparkling dark gray scales and glowing green eyes that stood several hands taller than Vâken. "I will not lie to you my brothers and sisters," the prince continued. "What we are about to see is unlike anything we have ever seen before in our lives. Our spies have reported that the irresponsible and greedy rulers have allowed Lord Bedlam to amass an army of creatures more powerful than previously thought."

Creatures? Kieron swallowed the fear building up inside. He looked over at Kealy and, with brows raised, she also looked concerned.

"But I assure you, we are not in this fight alone. The men and dwarves who value honor and life are out there, ready to join us, including Prince Peter and King Alexander of Illiath."

The riders cheered.

"And we have the great Dragon of the Forest on our side!" He removed his sword and raised it high into the air. The riders cheered even louder. "Onward toward victory!"

"Yes!" Kieron raised his arm into the air. "To victory for Vulgaard!"

"Here we go," Kealy said.

Prince Thætil heeled his dragon's side and shot into the air, followed by all the riders, including Kieron and Kealy.

Once in the frigid air, Kieron and Kealy flew over the various lands below. Farmlands, hamlets, rivers, and forests passed by them as the sun rose higher into the sky.

Suddenly, below them were the ruins of the once mighty palace of King Alexander, demolished by the illegitimate Duke of Illiath.

The once friend of Prince Peter, Sir William betrayed the king and worked with Lord Bedlam to betray King Alexander, the man he once saved, and destroy his kingdom.

Kieron thought about Prince Thurdin and wondered if he could do the same thing to the palace at Vulgaard. Was Sir William under a spell, too?

"Look, Kieron!" Kealy shouted and stirred Kieron from his thoughts.

She pointed to the troops landing by the ruins. They followed suit and landed their dragons.

"Come, let's go see what's happening." Kealy hopped off her dragon and removed her sword. Kieron did the same thing.

The elfin guards motioned for everyone to hide in the bushes and remain silent. Kieron and Kealy obeyed. The bushes lined the open field facing the ruins of the palace.

"What are we hiding from?" Kieron whispered.

"If I knew, I would tell you." Kealy stared at the empty field.

Kieron thought about telling Prince Thætil about Prince Thurdin's strange condition. But how could he? Would anyone believe him?

"Shh!" Kealy pointed to the field.

When Kieron saw what she pointed at, his eyes widened with fear.

Several of Sir William's men rode up to the ruins with swords drawn.

"They were spotted here," one man said to the other. "Elves on dragons. Search the area!"

He and the others rode horses that had banners draped over their backs underneath the saddles. The banners had the Duke's emblem painted on them, a crude depiction of a wolf devouring a lion. Kieron understood its meaning. Everyone knew the lion was King Alexander's symbol. The men trotted on their horses closer to the stacks of limestone bricks and twisted rods of metal where the gate to the palace of Illiath had once stood.

"Keep watch here," the leader ordered the other men as he galloped off toward the eastern side of the palace.

"Kieron," Kealy whispered. "Over there."

She nodded her head toward Prince Thætil, who held up his hand, signaling the attack. But the elves next to Kieron and Kealy motioned for them to hold back.

"Second wave," one elf whispered to Kieron and Kealy. "Stand fast."

Kealy turned to Kieron and nodded. "Understand?"

"We go in after the prince?"

She nodded and smiled. "Steady."

A few more stressful seconds passed as they hid in the bushes and waited for the men to relax and dismount their horses. Once they did, the battle began.

"Attack!" Prince Thætil shouted, and almost one hundred elves and their dragons emerged from the bushes that lined the field, catching the men off guard. Arrows flew through the air and hit a few of the men. The others drew swords to fight, but dragon flame put that idea to an end.

Kealy and Kieron rushed out to fight what was left, but the other men galloped away in fear for their lives. The prince ordered elves on dragons to follow them and finish them off.

"Well, that's done." Kealy wiped her hands and sheathed her sword.

A few crows overhead cawed and circled them. "Uh oh." Kieron frowned.

"What is it?" Kealy glanced up and saw the crows. "It's just some birds."

"Not just birds. Crows." Kieron ran to the prince. "Bedlam's spies."

"Prince Prince Thætil!" Kieron shouted. But the prince's guards stopped him.

"What do you want, boy?" one guard asked.

"I need to tell the prince about the crows!" Kieron said between breaths.

"Crows?" Prince Thætil made his way over to Kieron.

He bowed. "Yes, Your Highness. We spotted several circling above."

"We must leave now." Prince Thætil searched the skies. "Thank you, young Kieron. Everyone, move out!"

After Kieron explained to the prince that crows had been spotted, he watched the prince order everyone back on their dragons. They all took off to head to the Dragon Forest.

"Spies?" Kealy shouted at Kieron as they flew.

"Yes. Lord Bedlam's spies. He now knows where we are and what we've just done."

Toward the east, the fire of Hildron burned. The dark castle was Lord Bedlam's, constructed at the base of the Black Hills..

"He'll send his fighters soon," Kieron shouted.

But Kealy's face turned pale, as if drained of all blood.

"What is it?" Kieron asked. When he turned, he saw what had alarmed her.

Coming toward them were hundreds of Bedlam's Baroks flying on their dragons. These grotesque mutations of men and beast were Bedlam's failed attempt to breed men and dragons into some sort of superior fighting creatures to do his bidding. Instead, the mutations were simply monsters, trained to kill at Bedlam's command.

"What are those things coming toward us?" Kieron shouted.

"Draw your sword and get ready to fight!" Kealy ordered.

Kieron obeyed and leaned close to Vâken's neck. "Now is our chance. You fly, and I'll slash at them with my sword. You use your fire as you see fit. We can do this together!" he told his dragon.

And together they headed into the fray, slashing at Barok legs and arms as they flew past. Dragon fire pierced the air, causing many elves and Baroks to spin out of control on their dragons.

"Kieron!" a familiar voice shouted.

He turned to see his friends, Thyler, Aerin, and Yon riding their dragons.

Thyler shot an arrow into the side of a Barok's dragon. The beast screamed and fell to the ground, where elves attacked the Barok, killing it.

"Well done!" Kieron shouted.

Together, they dove to attack more Baroks. The mutant creatures were strong, but not very adept at fighting in the air. Kieron slashed at the arm of one Barok, who snarled at him and turned his dragon to burn Kieron. Vâken ducked out of the way in time and flew away. But the Barok and its dragon chased them.

"Come on!" Kieron shouted. "Follow me." He nudged Vâken to go even faster toward a waiting Thyler and Arein.

As they approached, Thyler loaded his bow, and Aerin's dragon prepared to spit its fire. When the Barok saw this, it pulled back on the reins, stopping its dragon. But it was too late. Thyler and Aerin took off after it to kill it.

"Good boy," Kieron said to Vâken.

An arrow whizzed by his head and he ducked just in time. He turned to see a wild-eyed Prince Thurdin on his dragon, loading another arrow into his bow.

"No," Kieron said and ordered Vâken to dive. He did and missed the other arrow. Kieron glanced behind to see Thurdin following them, and fast. His dragon was larger and more powerful, but Vâken was smaller and more agile, so Kieron led them away into the nearby forest.

He leaned in close to avoid the low lying branches. Vâken easily navigated through the trees, coming so close to the ground to splash the pond water with his belly. Kieron turned to see Prince Thurdin using his sword to slice away the branches. He and his dragon were catching up. Kieron had an idea. He knew the land better than the prince or the mutant creatures.

"To the river," he ordered Vâken. He quickly turned left and flew toward the raging river ahead. Thurdin kept going straight because his dragon couldn't make the turn in time, but Kieron knew they would catch up. He also knew larger branches hung low along the river. He and his siblings used to dangle from them to catch fish.

As they approached, he could hear the rushing water. "Over there," he said, and Vâken obeyed. Sure enough, Thurdin and his dragon appeared. "Whoa!" Kieron shouted as he and Vâken made their way nearer the trees.

Thurdin and his dragon followed.

Kieron smiled because his trap was working. "Keep going!"

Vâken did as he was told and flew above the riverbed, ducking under tree branches with Thurdin's dragon catching up.

Up ahead, Kieron saw the perfect opportunity to get rid of the prince. He'd use the same method he had tried with Aislinn in the forest near home.

As they approached a rather low branch, he timed it perfectly. Reaching up, he grabbed it and left the saddle. Vâken continued on his way. When Thurdin and his dragon approached, Kieron let go of the branch and landed behind Thurdin on top of his dragon.

"What the—"

Before the prince could react, Kieron shoved him into the icy river water below, just as Aislinn had taught him.

CHAPTER 16

P rince Thurdin's dragon began to slow, so Kieron reached up and grabbed another low lying branch. He hid in the tree atop the branch, and waited for Vâken to return. When he did, Kieron hopped on and away they flew out of the woods, leaving Thurdin's dragon searching for the prince in the river water as it flowed.

Kieron landed Vâken near where Kealy and her dragon waited with the others.

"You escaped!" Kealy rushed to him.

"I used the ol' branch tactic that Aislinn taught us." He raised his arms above his head. "Victorious!"

"Well done." Kealy patted his back.

"Good job, brother," Théan said. He and his friend Geraint approached.

"Did you see action here as well?" he asked.

"Oh yes." Thean pointed to his arm where an arrow had grazed him, tearing his tunic. "We're heading over to hear our orders from Prince Thaetil."

Kealy waved at their backs. "We'll be here, resting."

Kieron stretched his back. "Oh, my muscles are sore. It seems to me we all were lucky to—" Kieron fell to the ground, screaming.

"Kieron!" Kealy shouted and saw the arrow protruding from Kieron's leg. She jerked around to see a Prince Thurdin fly off, atop his dragon. "No!"

Kealy ran to her dragon, climbed onto his back, and flew off with her bow in her hand.

"Kealy, no!" Kieron shouted after her. But it was no use. She was bent on vengeance.

Kieron took hold of the arrow in his thigh and screamed from the pain. Théan rushed over to him.

"Kieron, what happened?" He inspected the arrow deep within his brother's leg.

"I...I don't know. It came out of nowhere." Kieron grimaced.

"Can you stand?" Théan blew his white hair out of his eyes and tried to lift his brother. "We've got to get you to the apothecary. But he's over by Prince Thætil's men."

"No!" Kieron shouted. "I can't move." He tried to sit up. "Kealy..."

"What about Kealy?" Théan asked with furrowed brow.

"She flew off to kill Prince Thurdin, who shot me. Go stop her!" Kieron motioned for Théan to go.

"Not until I get you help," he replied and searched the area for help.

"The healing powder," Kieron said, sweat dripping down his face. "Find some."

Théan twisted his head in confusion. "What is this powder?"

"I know what he means," said Geraint.

"Then go find it!" Théan shoved Geraint. "He's losing blood!"

Kieron searched the skies for his friend, but the sweat in his eyes burned. "Ah, I can't see." He wiped his eyes. "Where is Kealy? Can you see her?"

Théan turned and looked throughout the sky for Kieron's friend. "No! I don't see her yet. But I will keep looking for—" Théan's eyes grew large. "There! There she is!" He pointed.

Kieron's eyes followed his brother's arm and spotted Prince Thurdin, chasing Kealy and her dragon.

"I must help her." Kieron struggled to stand. "Vâken!"

"You can't, you fool. You're losing too much blood." Théan shoved his brother back down.

Geraint ran to them, carrying a small pouch. "Here." He held it out. "Pour some into your palm."

Théan obeyed.

Next, Geraint poured some water into the powder. "Mix it well."

Théan did and then spread the paste onto Kieron's wound. "On my count, I will remove the arrow."

Kieron felt the burning sensation in his thigh. "It's working. I can feel the paste working."

"Alright. Prepare yourself." Théan took hold of the arrow. "Ready?"

Kieron winced and then looked into the sky for Kealy. *I've got to help her.* "Yes! Do it!"

"One...two...three!" Théan pulled the arrow out of Kieron's thigh with one yank.

Kieron screamed and fell backwards, gripping his leg.

Théan and Geraint quickly spread more of the paste onto the wound as it healed.

Kieron lay back with closed eyes, breathing heavily. The burning sensation spread, but the pain diminished.

"Kieron, it's working." Théan smiled. "It's working! Your leg is healing."

"Good." Kieron stood. "Vâken!" His dragon flew over. "We've got to help Kealy. Let's go."

Théan and Geraint hopped onto their dragons and joined Kieron in the sky.

Together, they searched for their friend but couldn't see her.

"The forest." Kieron pointed toward the thin trees. The three elves flew into the forest, dodging branches. They shot high above the trees, searching for their friend.

"Look out!" Théan moved his body out of the way just in time to miss an arrow.

Kieron turned and saw Prince Thurdin flying toward him atop his dragon. It opened its mouth and spewed a line of fire right at him. Kieron tugged on Vâken's horns and turned to the left. They escaped the flames.

His dragon has its fire glands. Kieron flew out of the forest and turned around to see Prince Thurdin fast approaching. He shouted dragonspeak to the prince's dragon, but it growled back that it was already free.

This dragon is not a slave. Kieron's eyes filled with fear. *This dragon was trained to fight.*

"Come on, Vâken," Kieron shouted. The two spun over the fields, hoping to lose the prince and his dragon, but it didn't work.

More fire shot at them, almost sending Kieron to the ground.

"Hang on!" Théan shouted to his brother.

A line of fire came from Théan's dragon, scaring off the prince for a moment. Geraint shot an arrow at him, but it missed. Théan loaded his bow and took aim, but the prince jerked his dragon around. The three elves and their dragons followed after him.

"We've got him on the run now!" Théan shouted.

Yes, Kieron thought. He leaned in close to Vâken's neck and urged him to fly faster. The dragon obeyed and flapped his wings. Kieron squinted his eyes in the wind and searched the area for Kealy. *Where is she? She's got to be around here some—*

And that's when he spotted her.

"No!" Kieron jerked on Vâken's horns to get him to slow down. He squawked in confusion and beat his wings. "I know, I know I told you to fly faster. But I've spotted Kealy."

He turned Vâken around and landed him near Kealy's lifeless body, lying on the field.

"Kealy!" Kieron ran to her and scooped her head into his hands. But her eyes remained closed. "Kealy, are you alright?" He lay his head onto her chest, but heard no breathing. "No, Kealy. Breathe. Please breathe. You can't be dead. You just can't."

He heard dragons roaring above him and glanced up in time to see Théan and Geraint shoot two arrows into some Baroks, sending him to their deaths. Geraint shot more arrows into the chests of the dragons.

The battle was over.

"What happened?" Théan's dragon landed. He hopped off it and ran over to Kieron.

"I don't know. I found her like this," he cried, cradling her head in his hands. Her eyes remained tightly closed.

"Kealy!" Kieron shouted to his friend.

Théan took Kealy's wrist and waited for a pulse. There was none. He ran his hands over her torso, but found no open wound. He squeezed her chest and heard a crack. Exhaling in frustration, he looked at Kieron. "Her ribs are broken. She must have fallen off her dragon."

"It's over there." Geraint pointed to dead dragon's body. Several arrows protruded from Söen's belly.

"Oh no," Kieron cried. Tears flowed from his eyes, blinding him from the sight of his dead friend. But in his mind, he could see his sister Aislinn's face as if she were alive and before him again.

And then he saw her lifeless body lying on the ground of Duggan's Crevice on that fateful day.

"No!" he had shouted as he watched his older sister fall to her death. "Aislinn…"

Kieron buried his head into Kealy's side and wept.

"I'm sorry I failed you. I'm so sorry. Please forgive me."

"Kieron." He heard Aislinn's voice. Kieron saw his sister in a vision, gently taking his hand. "You didn't fail me, you silly elf."

Kieron looked into his sister's green eyes. "I didn't?"

She shook her head. "I did what I was supposed to do. I saved you so you could go on to save our land."

"But I was the one fooling around. I should have—"

"Nonsense." Aislinn took her brother's face into her hands. "It was my time to go. Now I am in a place where I will ride dragons across the sky forever." She waved her hand through the air. "And, one day, you'll be with me."

Kieron smiled, trying to imagine the scene.

"But not for a long, long time. Alright?" Aislinn asked.

Kieron nodded.

"Don't leave me, Kealy. Not you, too."

Théan rubbed his brother's back.

"First Aislinn, and now Kealy…" Kieron gripped her tunic and pulled it to himself. "Not you, my friend."

Théan winced at the painful sight.

Geraint knelt down and removed the pouch. Théan spotted it. "Will it work?"

"Don't know, but it's worth a try." He handed it to Théan.

Kieron lift his head and wiped his face with his hand. "Yes, please. Try."

"But there's no wound to rub the paste into." Théan poured the powder into his hand. "Her wounds are inside."

"Maybe place some in her mouth?" Geraint asked.

Kieron begged. "Please…try." He gripped Kealy's tunic even tighter.

Théan and Geraint looked at each other and then made the paste with water from Geraint's leather pouch. Théan gently raised the paste to Kealy's colorless lips.

"No," Kieron said. "Let me."

He took some paste and, using his fingers, gently opened his friend's mouth. "Please let this work." He fed some of the paste to Kealy. "Please work."

The three elves waited, but nothing happened. Kieron fed her more paste and rubbed her neck, doing his best to make her swallow.

"It is no use. We were too late." Théan sat back and ripped some grass from the ground, tossing it aside in anger.

But Kieron continued to feed his friend the healing paste made from ground dragon horns. He leaned in close to Kealy's ear and whispered. "Kealy, listen to me. Do as I say. Listen to the dragonspeak deep within you, Kealy," he said. "Listen to the voice calling you back. Hear it, Kealy. You must listen to it."

He gently rubbed her belly, as though hoping the paste was making its way through her body. "Please work…" he muttered to no one. "Please let it work. Don't take my friend away from me. Please don't take my friend."

"I'm afraid it's no use," Geraint said. He stood and tossed his leather pouch to the ground. "We should get her back to her family."

Aislinn, Kieron thought. *If you can hear me, sister, tell Kealy to come back to us.*

"I know where they live." Théan began to stand. "I will take her there and tell them what happened."

*Please, Aislinn…*Kieron thought. *Please tell Kealy to come back.*

"Wait!" Kieron shouted and sat back.

Théan and Geraint fell to their knees next to Kealy's body. "What is it?" Théan asked.

Kealy's abdomen slowly rose and then fell.

"Kealy?" Kieron leaned in with weepy eyes. He watched for her eyes to open. "Are you there?"

She coughed, causing Théan and Geraint to whoop and jump around with joy, slapping each other on the back.

"What…what's happening?" Kealy said in a small voice. She slowly opened her eyes.

Kieron tossed his head back and laughed. "Thank you!" He searched the skies and caught a glimpse of sunlight peeking through the clouds"Thank you, Aislinn. Thank you."

Hobbling to a nearby pond, Kieron helped Kealy sit by the water's edge.

"Söen?" she asked.

Kieron shook his head. "I'm so sorry."

Kealy stared off into the distance.

"I'm sorry I wasn't there to help you, friend." Kieron sat next to her.

Kealy reached over and squeezed his hand. "You helped me, you silly elf."

Kieron chuckled. "That's what Aislinn used to call me."

Kealy playfully shoved him, making Kieron smile.

"Kealy," he asked. "What did you see?"

She drank some water from Geraint's water pouch. "What do you mean?"

"When you were…you know." Kieron watched the water lap against the pond's edge.

Kealy thought about it for a moment. "Well, I don't remember seeing anything at all. I remember falling to the ground, and then everything went dark."

Kieron listened.

"But I did hear something." Kealy turned to him.

"You did?"

Kealy nodded. "Yes. I heard faint voices."

Kieron faced her. "My voice?"

She nodded again.

"We were…I mean, I was crying out to you to come back." He lowered his eyes.

"I heard you." Kealy nudged him again. Then her face turned serious.

"What is it?"

"Then I heard another voice…"

Kieron sat up. "Yes?"

"It was very soft. Very quiet. I heard my name and someone telling me to go back, that it wasn't my time yet." She stared at the horizon. "It was so strange."

Kieron grinned widely, knowing it was Aislinn's voice Kealy had heard.

"Well, it's time to go. It will be dark soon. Are you okay to travel, Kealy?" Théan asked as he walked up behind them.

She rose and dusted off her tunic. "I am. In fact, I feel terrific."

Théan smiled. "That's good, considering you were dead just a few moments ago."

Kealy chuckled.

"You'll have quite the story to tell your parents and siblings." Théan winked.

"And the prince?" she asked.

"He got away, but don't worry," Théan said. "There will be many more chances to get him."

∽

Kieron and his friends would endure more battles in the war against Lord Bedlam, chronicled in many books about The Dragon Forest.

When the mission to rid the land of the evil Darkness did come to an end. Kieron, Kealy, and Théan had all successfully fought alongside many others, including Prince Peter of Illiath, who would soon be crowned king. But Kieron lamented the deaths of his friends, Thyler and Aerin.

In Vulgaard many months later, after the dead were buried and elves returned to their homes, the land healed and Kieron returned to his family in Glouslow to help them plant and harvest crops. Théan married and purchased a farm of his own nearby.

But after two more years had passed, an edict went throughout the land to resume the Dragon Games of old.

Kieron felt it was time for the Dragon Games to resume, but this time, with the permission of the dragons.

He organized a group of elfin leaders to go and speak with the dragons. While some remained in the plains and mountain regions, some did want to compete in the games.

Kieron vowed the games would honor the dragons and respect their skills. They would be celebrated and not controlled.

He found himself preparing Vâken, once again for the tournament; this time, as an instructor who had flown with the queen's Dragon Riders.

"You sure you have everything you'll need?" his father asked.

"Yes, sir."

"Good. Vâken's a fine dragon. I see you are taking these young dragons along with you."

"Yes. Vâken and I have worked with them. They are ready."

"If you trained them, then they'll do well in the tournament. Fly true." He patted Vâken's snout.

"Always." Kieron smiled at his loyal dragon, remembering their adventures.

"Hello!" Kealy waved from atop her dragon. She landed nearby. "It's been many months of training dragons as an instructor. Are you ready to head out to the games?"

Kieron hopped onto Vâken. "Of course!"

He nudged his dragon and waved goodbye to his family. "Goodbye, Father!"

"Be safe!"

Kieron and Kealy once again soared through the air toward the titling fields at the base of the Ranvieg Mountains.

As they landed, the once ominous mountain range now was covered in wildflowers and dragons munching on the fresh green grass.

"What a sight!" Kieron shouted.

"Quite a difference a couple of years makes." Kealy hopped off her dragon and walked her toward the line of competitors.

A group of elves ran over to Kieron and began cheering for him and Vâken.

Kealy stepped aside to allow Kieron the chance to enjoy the moment.

Kieron chuckled as he remembered the time when he had watched his brother's adoring fans surround him with cheers. Kieron had whispered to Vâken long ago, *"One day, that'll be us. We'll be winners of the Dragon Games and have all the adoring fans."*

He shook the hands of the young elves as they ask him their questions and told him how much they admired him.

After the kids returned to the field, Kealy made her way over to Kieron. "How's it feel?"

He shrugged. "Good, I guess."

"Kieron and Vâken"

Ahead of them was Memorial Way, the path dedicated to those lost in the war with Bedlam.

"It's hard to believe what we all endured to get to this moment." Kieron's eyes shone as he thought about the loss of his friends, Thyler, Aerin, and Yon, who had perished in the battle with Lord Bedlam's fighters. Plaques that honored their service hung on wooden poles that lined the special path. He stared into the names of his friends, brave young men who had fought hard for freedom.

"So much loss." Kieron sighed. "I can't believe they are gone. I can still hear their laughter." He ran his finger along Thyler's name. "He longed to make the people of Heinland's Gate proud as a Dragon Rider, just like his brothers had."

"He did." Kealy placed her hand onto his shoulder. "I know you miss them, but they are here with us now...in spirit."

Kieron nodded.

"They'd want you to train these young elves well, you know." She smiled. "So they, too, can one day ride with the queen's Dragon Riders."

"I know."

A few elves approached Kieron. "Here, take these young dragons to the stalls. They are ready for riders," he ordered them.

He watched as the elves led the dragons away. "This time, the dragons are here by choice."

"Exactly." Kealy patted his shoulder.

"Brother!" Kieron turned around to see his younger sister land her dragon nearby.

"Everleigh!" He trotted over to her and took the bridle of her dragon into his hands to steady it.

"I am so glad you are here, Everleigh." Kealy made her way over.

"Are you ready?" Kieron asked his sister.

Wearing Aislinn's old leather breastplate and tunic, Everleigh nodded enthusiastically. Her white hair was braided down her back, and attached to her saddle was Kieron's old quiver of arrows.

"You look ready," he said. "And so does Fawn."

The little dragon chirped and blinked her eyes in the bright sun.

Kealy stepped back and studied the dragon. "Is this the same dragon that was—"

"In the dungeon, yes." Kieron nuzzled the little dragon.

"She came to us one day!" Everleigh giggled. "Kieron spotted her in our field and now she's part of our family. She's mine now. All mine."

"Her wings healed nicely and she's quite fast now." Kieron patted Fawn on the head. "And brave."

"Alright, Everleigh," Kealy began. "Dismount and walk your dragon over to where the others are. Those are your competitors. Study them well."

Everleigh obeyed and walked Fawn to the field.

"Are *you* ready?" Kealy turned toward Kieron.

"Absolutely." He lifted his chin and grinned proudly.

"Then do them proud. Fly strong and fly true. Alright?" Kealy turned to leave.

"Always."

Kieron sat on Vâken, high in the saddle. He secured his boots into the stirrups and gripped tightly to the reins. He rubbed Vâken's neck. "Let's show them what dragon riding looks like."

Together, Kieron and Vâken flew to the tilting field and waved his red flag. "Competitors, mount your dragons." His job would be to lead the competitors through the course while they desperately tried to capture his flag. The one to capture it would be declared winner of this event. But there would be many more events to follow.

He saw Everleigh grip the reins and lean close to Fawn's neck, just as he had taught her. *Will she be the winner? She certainly is capable.*

Kieron smiled at the sight of her and all the other excited elves atop their dragons. They were free dragons at the games of their own volition. They, too, wanted a chance to fly with the Dragon Riders.

"To your marks!" Kieron cried to the many competitors.

Everleigh nudged her dragon to make her way over to the line where all the other competitors stood. Some were older and bigger than she was. But she had grown much over the last few years.

She'll do fine, Kieron thought. *She can hold her own.*

Vâken squawked.

"Are you remembering our time training for the games?" he asked his loyal dragon, hovering over the field.

"Get set!" Kieron shouted to the competitors.

He leaned forward and ran through the course inside his head. Then he glanced over to the Ranvieg Mountains and remembered how he and his friends had escaped with the help of the dragons and Dangler, the Dragon Master. Never in a million years did Kieron ever think he would have made it out, let alone fly his dragon into battle with other fighters from so many lands.

He knew in his heart what his purpose was. All that came before was what made him ready. He leaned close to Vâken's neck and listened to his breathing. He closed his eyes and visualized them flying over Vulgaard with Aislinn on her dragon in peace.

And then he opened his eyes.

"Go!"

THE END

ABOUT TH THE AUTHOR

R. A. Douthitt is a writer and an artist.
Illustrating the books for *The Elves of Vulgaard* series has
been a rewarding experience for her.
She is the award-winning author of *The Dragon Forest* trilogy and
The Children series, winner of the Moonbeam Children's Book Award-
Bronze Medal for Best Book Series.
For more information about R. A. Douthitt, visit her website.
www.artbyruth.com

Made in the USA
Las Vegas, NV
09 September 2021

29926331R00118